OF
SERPENT
BORN

To THE MOTHER
and to my loving husband

Thank you...
to the Midwives who helped Birth this book,
Olivia and all at Ragged Bears.

OF SERPENT BORN

J. ZACHARIAS

Ragged Bears

First published in 2018 by Ragged Bears Ltd

Sherborne, DT9 3PH

www.ragged-bears.co.uk

ISBN: 9781857144727

1 2 3 4 5 6 7 8 9 10

Printed in Poland

A CIP catalogue record for this book is available
from the British Library

Printed using sustainably sourced paper

…and The Serpent hissed to me,
"before you sleep tonight,
you must know, I will take you to a place
where black cats lead the way
and snakes of copper and gold
shed their skins upon your feet."
…and The Serpent hissed to me,
"before you sleep tonight,
you must know, I will take you to a place
where owls do not hoot
but stare at me and you
amid whispering, moon-veiled shadows."
…and The Serpent hissed to me,
"before you sleep tonight,
you must know, I will take you to a place
where faceless beings with shimmering wings
dance demented to ancient rhymes
upon luminous waters of silvery black."
…and The Serpent hissed to me,
"before you sleep tonight,
you must know, I will take you to a place.
You will meet The Hidden One.
It has your face . . . shall we?"

YORK

CHAPTER ONE

The pregnant moon reflected a shadowy pearl hue upon the silver waters. Her bare feet felt cold against the soft, damp soil of the riverbank as she followed the pretty, slim black cats with electric yellow eyes. Their unusually long, black tails flicked urgently against the cool twilight wind. In the distance, she heard the faint echo of incomprehensible chants. Suddenly, the cats stopped at the edge of the riverbank. With fiery eyes ablaze, they faced her, hissing.

Unsure, she paused.

It was then the waters began to churn.

And she awoke...

"Good morning, princess," Durga kissed her daughter on the forehead as she served green tea and muesli for breakfast.

"Mmm..." mumbled Anitha, unenthusiastically.

She sipped her tea, watching the birds peck the seeds from the bird feeder. The dining area faced the extensive kitchen window, treating her to a lovely view of the back garden. Bird watching calmed her nerves. So did the river.

"Ready for school?" Durga knew her daughter always completed her homework and studied for tests and examinations without needing to be told but she asked anyway. It is what mothers did.

Anitha nodded, her long, slanting eyes still glued to the birds. "I'll walk to school, mum."

It was a dry day with the sun shining a gentle glow. There was no need to object. Durga watched her daughter eat her gluten-free Swiss muesli. Anitha's skin and moods had considerably improved after being diagnosed with celiac disease and being put on a gluten-free and dairy-free diet.

Durga laid an elaborately designed card on the table. It was a wedding invitation. "Your cousin Chandra is getting married this weekend."

Anitha released a heavy sigh.

"You don't have to attend," Durga added, kindly.

"And leave you to the vultures?" Anitha savoured the last bit of her muesli.

"Your father's family can be difficult..." agreed Durga, helping herself to another cup of tea.

"They are mean and they hate you because you

poached one of their kind. They hate me more because I am the half-breed of this unholy union…and they hate us multiplied by a hundred because dad is…" Anitha choked on the word that refused to be said aloud.

Tearfully, Durga rose to embrace her daughter.

Anitha hugged her mother back.

It was a twenty-minute walk to school. The sun kissed her face, comforting her grief with its warm touch. She was grateful for the time spent in solitary walks; It allowed her to think. She approached the village park with its tall trees and clipped lawn. Some students of St Anne's were strolling leisurely, absorbed in their private conversations. Others were busy with their phones.

Anitha watched the birds and squirrels and rabbits go about their respective routines. Fishing a handful of nuts from her pocket, she knelt, flattening her palms out on the grass. Two squirrels came by and snatched them. Smiling, she resumed her walk.

She contemplated last night's dream: it was vivid and the colours were sharper than normal. Even now, in the reality of daylight, she could hear the hiss of the black cats in her ears. Their gleaming, yellow eyes were burned in her mind.

Turning a corner, she neared the school gates.

"Ugly!" someone yelled before breaking out into a fit of laughter.

"Freak!" another joined in.

"You don't belong here!" a third snarled.

With her head lowered and her schoolbag pressed tightly against her chest, Anitha dragged her feet towards the school grounds, her heart racing fearfully.

CHAPTER TWO

On her hands and knees, she crawled through an endless cave. Slithering creatures accompanied her journey as long-tailed panthers bared their fangs, galloping ahead with ease and grace. A ray of moonlight finally illuminated the darkness as she heard the bubbling of a stream. At the mouth of the cave, she stood scanning the landscape of weeping willows and a cascade of thundering waterfall of turquoise gold. Her feet moved closer to the river. With slight trepidation, she dipped her naked toes in the waters. It felt cool and fresh. Bewitched, she continued to fix her gaze on the waterfall.

Suddenly, the waters beneath her feet began to swirl and churn. She slipped, her feet now completely immersed in water. The river rose, caressing and encircling her up and up to her knees.

A bell rang.

Anitha woke up.

The bell was still ringing.

The clock on the wall displayed half past three in the morning. She rubbed her eyes. Daylight was seeping dimly through the curtains. It was midsummer and in July, she would turn sixteen.

The sound of the ringing bell stirred her further to waking. It was Saturday. As far as Anitha could remember, her mother had always performed morning prayers on early morning weekends. Anitha herself was never coerced into the ritual. Enforced faith never did create a happy human, mum told her.

However, today, she was curious.

Durga walked around the house bearing a small tray of incense, softly ringing a silver bell and chanting mantras quietly. At three in the morning, she had risen, bathed in sea salt and helped herself to a hot cup of spiced tea before preparing for the puja (prayer). She turned to enter the dining room.

"Good morning, mum!"

"Oh, Anitha!" Durga raised her eyebrows, surprised. "What are you doing up so early? Go back to bed…"

Dressed in her pyjamas, Anitha shook her head. "I just want to see…besides, I am wide awake."

Durga paused. "All right, then. I would advise you

to take a quick shower before you follow me about..."

Anitha opened her mouth to protest but seeing her mother's stern, unblinking eyes, she climbed back upstairs.

By the time Anitha was downstairs, her mother had finished burning incense in the living room, dining room and the kitchen. Silently, Anitha trailed after her mother as she completed the rooms upstairs. She then accompanied her mother outside.

The morning was cold and a slight drizzle had begun. Durga made her way down the steps to the riverbank where the willow trees swayed in the early morning mist. It was a picture worth painting but Anitha was no artist. From the top of the wooden steps, she watched her mother kneel before one of the many trees and lay a small metal bowl of milk infused with turmeric. Beside the bowl, she laid a few coins. Lowering her head, she brought her palms together and muttered rhyming alien words. Once finished, she looked up, smiling at her daughter.

"Let's have breakfast. I'll make some pancakes!"

Durga flipped the rice pancakes before drizzling maple syrup over them. Anitha set cups and saucers and the pot of lemon verbena and ginger tea on the table before laying the plates and knives and forks.

"So, have you picked out an outfit for the wedding

today?" Durga laid the pancakes on the plates.

Glumly, Anitha nodded. It was clear she was an unwilling participant in the celebratory occasion.

"I hope it is colourful and shining..." Durga popped a slice of pancake into her mouth.

"Whatever..." came the dull reply. Anitha sipped her tea, which was warm and soothing. "Mum, can you order some books for me from Amazon?"

"What sort of books?"

"It's for my geography project. We are supposed to pick one of the elements of nature and discuss the ecological impact of human activities on it."

"What element did you pick?"

"Water."

Durga kept silent, her eyes keenly observing her daughter.

"I've already picked a title."

"Oh?" Durga placed another pancake on Anitha's plate.

"Project Anahita..." Anitha beamed.

"That's a gorgeous name!" complimented Durga.

"Who gave me my name, mum? Was it dad or you?"

"Your grandma...my mother."

"The one living in Kerala?"

Durga nodded.

"Did you know, mum, that my name Anitha

is a derivative of Anahita? Like Anne and Anna or Hannah…apparently, Anahita is the name of an old, ancient Persian Goddess – she is also referred to as the Lady of the Waters…ancient people worshipped her for fertility and protection. In ancient Hebrew, she is considered an angel of fertility and waters. How cool is that?"

Durga had stopped eating. She stared intently at her daughter who was blossoming each day into a young woman. "Very cool."

"Because of her association with the water element and being my namesake, I thought the project title was perfect. Besides, I like the fact that she is a Goddess. I find it rather empowering, you know, being a girl and all."

"I'm proud of you, princess."

"So, I have a list of books I need to research, mum."

"Give me the list and I'll get on it instantly."

CHAPTER THREE

It was an attack on the senses.

Decked in gleaming gold, silver and precious gems, women and girls adorned in traditional attires, sashayed in shimmering rainbow hues. Unlike Anitha and her mum, her dad's family were large-boned with hawk-like noses, considerably taller with pale skin, light hair and piercing eyes. Drumbeats and trumpet sounds and the constant chatter of people and cries of toddlers and babies deafened the ears. The drifting smoke of incense, with scents of rose, jasmine and sandalwood, was saturating the air with its heady scent.

Anitha nibbled a sweetmeat. It was milky, nutty and moist with thick syrup. She leaned against the wall. Those her age brushed past her, busy in their own little world of gossip and phones. Nobody bothered to include her in their circle. Even the elders of the community measured her with their unwelcoming stare.

Anitha did not mind. She was used to being by herself.

"The parking was a nightmare," apologised Durga as she made her appearance. She smiled at her husband's oldest sister, Sushmita. The goodwill gesture was not returned.

Shrugging her shoulders, Anitha resumed nibbling the sweetmeat.

"The temple ceremony is about to begin..." Durga announced, smoothing down her daughter's stray curl.

"Whatever..." Anitha muttered.

The wedding dais was elaborately decorated with strings of multi-coloured fresh flowers, dark green leaves and semi-precious stones. Polished trays of offerings and gifts symbolising prosperity and fertility were on shameless display. They included bananas, saffron-infused milk in miniature crystal cups, jars of Himalayan honey, a variety of nuts and seeds, neatly stacked notes tied in gold threads, pyramid piles of gold coins, intricately designed jewellery, silken saris and shawls. The bride, Chandra, Anitha's father's niece, was hunched over, veiled and weighed down by the thick garb of crimson red and peacock blue. Gold, silver, rubies and sapphires embellished every inch of her slender frame.

She was only twenty-two.

I'm never going to get married, thought Anitha as she impatiently crossed and uncrossed her ankles. *I'm going to study really hard to get a scholarship to Cambridge. Slavery is not an option for me. Husbands and children are a trap to put women in their place.* She observed the women around her, their lives worn out by the never-ending needs of men and children.

Agitated by the lengthy drone of the priests as they babbled holy words of matrimonial blessings, she gulped down the remaining mineral water. The urge to pee kicked in.

"Mum, I'm off to the loo," she whispered.

Durga turned sideways to let Anitha pass.

The crowd was coming and going. Anitha pushed her way to the lobby where many more guests were loitering about. Ladies were exchanging the latest updates on fashion, a couple of women were breastfeeding, older men were drinking chai and youngsters were fiddling with their phones.

She followed the sign to the lavatory. Inside, there was a group of girls giggling, talking about boys as they applied fresh coats of lipstick and brushed down their long, thick hair. One of them was the bride's little sister, Uma. Uma was already sixteen. Anitha hesitated to enter but she was desperate. In her heart, she prayed to whatever power she thought could protect her.

As soon as she stepped in, silence fell.

"Look what we have here…" sneered Uma, her pink lips twisting in scorn. The silver bangles on her corpse-white skin jingled as she waved a long, pink manicured forefinger at Anitha.

Ignoring Uma, Anitha picked the nearest cubicle.

Instantly, Uma barred her way. "Killer…" she spat.

"Leave her alone, Uma," one of the girls warned. "It's your sister's wedding. You don't want trouble."

"She killed her father and she killed my grandmother. She is a curse. I was denied my uncle and my grandmother because this thing was born…" Uma's face assumed a feral expression. "She is trouble." Uma edged closer to Anitha, her unwavering mean eyes, narrowing. "The world should be rid of you…and your whore of a mother…"

Anitha snapped. Fury roared inside her. Her body buzzed as though an electrical current shot through it. "You brahmin bitch!" Her hand curled around Uma's throat, gripping it, squeezing it tightly. Even when Uma's eyes bulged and rolled upwards, Anitha refused to let go. Screams and shouts blasted through the air. The girls began frantically pulling the adversaries apart.

Still, Anitha held on.

Veins throbbed against Uma's fair temples. Eventually, someone jumped on Anitha's back, biting hard into her cheeks, pulling her hair apart.

Anitha released her prey.

Stumbling forward, Uma choked and coughed. Her friends gathered around her, mouthing words of concern as she collapsed on the floor.

Her body, still buzzing, Anitha freed herself from the circle of girls and spun round, running like hell.

The ritual was almost completed. Guests whistled and clapped as they threw coloured rice on the newlyweds wishing them fertility and wealth.

It was time for the bride and groom to seek blessings from friends and family. Durga got up from her seat and joined the queue that led to the dais. In her hand was a red envelope with five hundred pounds gift money. The bride and groom were now prostrating before the patriach of the family, her father-in-law. It was he who had sent her the invitation.

They had always been on amiable terms but over the years his daughters had cast a considerable influence upon his life. They spoke over the telephone a few times a year. That was all. Anitha addressed her grandfather civilly. He was proud of her academic success.

"The smartest in the family," he once boasted very quietly on the telephone.

Durga had smiled.

Now, seated in his wheelchair, he was a mere husk of his former self. He was too weak to raise his hands to bless the newlyweds.

"What do you think you are doing?"

Durga turned. It was Sushmita, her sister-in-law. "I'm in the queue to bless the couple."

"I don't think so." Sushmita glowered. Pearls studded her long, brown hair tied in a neat bun at the nape of her neck. Light, grey eyes flashed cruelly at Durga.

"Excuse me?"

"You heard me."

"I heard you."

"Leave your gift at the main table. Your blessings will not be required."

Open mouthed, Durga stared in disbelief. People around her were now paying attention to the unfolding scene. Nobody intervened.

"My father invited you. My sister Usha and I did not. It is her daughter's wedding. Please honour her wishes."

Someone tugged at Durga's sleeve.

It was Anitha. Her face was tear stricken. Distress puckered her face. "Mum, let's go home."

"Yes," Sushmita growled. "You take this curse with you."

Rage simmered through Durga's veins. "Anitha is my daughter."

"This creature swallowed my brother when she was

born and if he was not enough to feed her greed, she swallowed my mother…"

Durga slapped Sushmita.

Sushmita's milky cheeks turned a sharp red. The entire wedding hall descended into a hush for minutes before pandemonium broke out.

Fortunately, an elderly gentleman escorted Durga and Anitha safely out of the building.

CHAPTER FOUR

It was almost nine in the morning on the Sunday when Anitha woke up from her deep and uninterrupted sleep. Rubbing her eyes she threw the duvet aside, letting her legs dangle by the edge of the bed as she briefly recounted last evening's drama.

The old man in his Armani suit was kind enough to let her use the loo before seeing them drive off. Uma and her squad had left by then so she relished the peace in the cubicle while freely letting her tears flow. It certainly didn't help that it was the second day of her period. Mum always said that the hormones are all over the place during the time of the month but really? She had nearly choked Uma to death! What was all that about? Where did that rage come from? Goodness knows what would have happened if the other girls had not broken up the fight.

Anitha shuddered, imagining Uma crumpled on the floor with a broken neck?

Killer.

That was what Uma had accused her of.

First her dad, then her granny; Uma could have been next.

It was luck that saved Uma from the near self-fulfilling prophecy.

Luck of the stars.

Perhaps the community was right. Anitha was cursed. She was born under the wrong stars. Within three months of her birth, she had 'swallowed' her father, within six months, her granny...

Quietly, Anitha burst into tears wondering why on earth she was even born...

The front door was wide open when she came down the stairs. The late morning sun was shining a golden yellow across the hallway and the chirp of the birds rang through the air; a small token of consolation for her grieving heart.

Durga was sitting in the front porch, admiring her blooms of intense English gold marigolds, pink and white lupines, dark purple lavender, bright pink geraniums and the sweet scented trellis of honeysuckle against the willow fencing along the path to the driveway. Bees buzzed delightfully around this floral

Eden. Hoverflies embarked upon swift flights of fancy in acrobatic motions. A lone dragonfly with papery, radiant emerald green wings rested on the windowsill of the front window basking in the warmth of the sun. Two lemon white butterflies flitted from flower to flower before deciding on the bush of the heavily fragrant purple buddleia. Upon the cherry blossom tree, laden with ripening cherries, hung three bird feeders. A gathering of sparrows busily tucked into their snacks.

Anitha sat on the willow armchair beside her mother. "Sorry for not joining you for the dawn prayers."

"Faith is not to be enforced nor threatened upon, princess..." Durga kissed her daughter on the left cheek. "Here, I've some ginger tea and honey in the pot."

"Thanks, mum..." Anitha sat on the chair beside the table separating her from her mother. Between them, silence nestled for a few minutes. "Look, mum," Anitha started. "I'm sorry for yesterday..."

"Please..." Durga waved her left palm dismissively. "I should have known better than to display such violence on a happy occasion. I could not bear your aunt viciously insulting you...the mama bear in me just reared its ugly head, tooth and claw."

"I almost choked Uma to death...she called you names..."

Durga nibbled into her oat biscuit. "I am sorry

you had to…this will never happen again. It is the last straw. Them and their outmoded beliefs and bigotry can go to hell. It is people like them with their ingrained, insular system of caste and prejudice that cripple human evolution." A grim expression clouded Durga's face. "Your father was different." Her voice softened. "His heart was open and free, his mind wise and keen to listen."

Anitha did not respond. Her mother had a faraway look.

Anitha had no memory of her father. When she was a mere three months old, she and dad had met with an accident. Apparently, dad was on the wrong side of the lane. The wreck stole her father's life but she, the baby survived miraculously.

When she turned seven, strange dreams tormented her. She heard awful sounds of car crashes, the crunching of metal and bones, dying moans and in the waves of darkness, a loving voice call out her name. She would wake up with sweaty palms and palpitating heartbeats.

Nowadays, she cried a lot less. Maybe, once in a few months, a feeling of emptiness would sink in and the tears would just pour. She let them.

Sometimes, Anitha wondered if the whole world would have preferred it if her father had survived and not her. It was clear he was a well-loved man by family and friends and especially mum. After fifteen years, the pain of losing a man like her father was still raw in the hearts of all he left behind.

Suddenly, she felt sad. She felt sad for granddad who had lost his only son, sad for her aunts who had lost their favourite sibling and even sad for Uma and her cousins who were denied the best uncle in the world.

Anitha glanced towards her mother still lost in dusty memories of her one true love. Grief rippled through her limbs. "I'm so sorry…ma…" tears sprung in her eyes.

Startled from her melancholic contemplation, Durga jumped off her seat and knelt in front of her daughter, cradling her head in her arms. "Never apologise for living. Your life meant everything to him."

A breeze stirred in the garden as it blew through the rustling leaves and fragrant flowers, kissing their hair and faces with its warm gentleness.

CHAPTER FIVE

Anitha chewed the rubber end of her pencil. On the table in the dining room lay stacks of papers, three books and her laptop. Hesitantly, she scribbled a few lines in her notebook before cancelling the entire paragraph. How on earth was she to condense the impact of fracking by multi-national corporations on water contamination? Her project was limited to three thousand words. This was ridiculous. She was capable of completing an entire thesis.

Outside, the birds were merrily chirping. The day was warm and dry. Bees buzzed in a low hum. Lilacs frothed on the right side of the front lawn and the ray of late afternoon sunshine cast a buttery glow upon the room. Mum was at the nursery and rang to say she would be late. She loved working there, growing organic herbs and vegetables and organising creative willow workshops. The home itself was littered with mum's own willow works – baskets, coasters and table mats.

Sighing, she rose from the table. There was some quinoa salad from last night's dinner left in the refrigerator. A warm breeze blew in from the open bay window. A yawn released from her open mouth. All that reading and research was making her head sleepy. A nap was a good idea. The quinoa salad could wait. She made her way to the living room and stretched out on the sofa. Immediately, her eyes closed.

She heard a purr. The purr was deep and near.

Her limbs, now completely relaxed, shifted on the softness of the sofa. It felt almost like velvet beneath her sleeping body. She moved to her side and *suddenly, felt herself plunging into a shimmer of water. The purr was increasingly loud. Reaching out, her arms began to move in a swimming motion. All around her, minute stars of myriad hues glittered in twinkling flashes. Faint outlines of stark-white marbled pyramids, gemstone-encrusted palace domes and meandering pathways lined with sapphires and rubies wavered in slippery scenes before her eyes. Winged spectres wearing elfin features blinked curiously at her but she sensed no harm from them. Instead after a few moments of scanning her, their long, slim and supple slithering bodies spun round, flicking golden tails cheekily in her face before dissolving into the depths of the azure watery splendour. Ripples sparkled a turquoise sheen before being swallowed in a blanket of pillow-soft blackness.*

Once more, soft, silken hairs caressed her arms. The almost audible hum of purr bristled through her ears. A pair of citrine-yellow feline eyes stared unblinkingly at her.

"Ebony!"

Anitha jolted, wiping a trickle of saliva from the left corner of her mouth.

"Ebony!"

A black furry ball of creature leapt from her abdomen, landing gracefully on the intricately woven Egyptian carpet.

"Ebony!"

Rubbing her eyes, Anitha wondered at the unsolicited guest before her.

Lean and black, it resembled a miniature panther.

"You are beautiful!" exclaimed Anitha, lost in admiration.

"Ebony!"

Anitha giggled. "You naughty little beast!" She opened the front door and stepped into the porch. The black cat trailed behind, unperturbed. "Your cat's here!" she called out. Kneeling down to stroke the animal, she heard footsteps jog along the driveway before arriving on her garden path.

"There you are Ebony!" the boy sounded flustered.

Anitha looked up. Her face burned hotly.

He was tall, almost six-foot with an unruly mop of coppery-red wavy, hair flecked with hints of gold. His skin was a pale tan that shone with sweat. Emerald-green eyes smiled down at her. "I'm terribly sorry. She does that all the time when I'm out with her delivering...these..." Long legs strode towards her. Large, rough hands handed her a leaflet.

Anitha accepted his paper.

"I do odd jobs around gardens during summer holidays. Please feel free to contact me. I could do with the extra pocket money."

Anitha lowered her eyes.

"Thanks..." he said.

"What for?" Anitha asked, her mouth dry.

"Ebony...I worry...you know...sometimes she disappears for days and weeks."

"She's pretty." Anitha heard her heart thump rapidly.

"She's precious. She was my mum's..."

Detecting a tone of sadness, Anitha did not venture for details. "Ebony must have come through the open window of the dining room." She pointed to the left.

"She's not in a hurry to leave, I see," the boy laughed, watching his cat rubbing and scenting herself around the chairs and table in the porch. "Come on, Ebony," he whistled. "It's time for tea…"

Ebony purred, pressing and brushing her delicate black hairs against Anitha's calves before leaping across the threshold and disappearing among the hedges.

Grinning, the boy offered, "I'm Solomon."

The wind stilled.

Leaves stopped rustling.

Birds on trees peered down at her.

"Oh…" Anitha managed as he walked away.

Suddenly, for the first time in her life, Anitha felt her IQ plummet.

CHAPTER SIX

A vague disquiet sat uneasily in the air. Anitha shifted restlessly in her seat. Anxiety swept like a tidal wave deep inside her.

"Stop fidgeting." Mrs Halliwell removed her white-rimmed spectacles, revealing kind blue eyes. Tap. Tap. Tap. Long, pink manicured nails tapped impatiently on the oak wood, managerial-type table.

Anitha mumbled an apology. Her eyes met the potted aloe vera on the windowsill and the four-foot yucca plant standing sturdy in the corner of the principal's office. Their leaves were impressively green and healthy.

There was a knock at the door. Mr Peterson, the secretary, popped his head in. "Miss Durga is here."

"Thank you. Send her in." Mrs Halliwell returned her spectacles to their rightful place.

Moments later, Durga entered. It was clear from her reaction that Anitha's dishevelled appearance shocked her. Splotches of soil and mud stained her uniform of blue and white. Anitha's hair was unruly with blades of grass entangled in her curls. Long, red scratch marks marked the right side of her face.

"Oh my god, Anitha!" cried Durga.

"Have a seat, Miss Durga."

Durga nodded. Her arms reached out to clasp her daughter's hand.

"Trust me, she looks a lot better than her adversaries." Mrs Halliwell began.

"What? Anitha! What's all this about?" Durga looked at her daughter then the principal.

"Your daughter and three other girls in her class were involved in a fight."

"I didn't start it." Anitha whimpered.

"Your daughter has related her side of the story and I have also heard the other side. Violence will not be tolerated on school grounds, Miss Durga. We take this seriously." There was a pause. "However, having said that, I am aware that Anitha is a committed student who excels in her studies. Her teachers testify to her excellent behaviour and performance in classes. We are proud of students like Anitha. With her academic track record, she is eligible for the best colleges in this country. This incident is a setback for all of us." Mrs

Halliwell shook her head disappointedly. A blond curl strayed away from the pearl-blue butterfly pin that held the fringe.

Fear lodged in Anitha's throat.

"It is the school's decision that Anitha is suspended for a week."

"That's not fair! I didn't start the fight! They picked on me! They always pick on me! They tore my geography project papers and laughed! They hate me!" Tears flooded down Anitha's scratched cheeks and cut lips.

"Who? Why didn't you tell me that you were being bullied?" Durga let her daughter sob on her shoulders.

"Miss Anitha, if only you could have alerted us regarding this bullying, things would not have come to this." Mrs Halliwell sighed sympathetically. She liked Anitha. The girl was good and smart. There was nothing to not like about the child.

"Well, she's told you now..." Durga eyed the principal squarely.

"Yes, we have details noted from Anitha's testimony. The board will be conducting a review. Trust me, Miss Durga we will deal with the girls once the investigation is completed but for now, they too have been suspended but for longer. They will not be returning to school till after the summer holidays."

Anitha was still crying.

Mrs Halliwell poured a jug of water into a glass and handed it over to her. "Drink this," she said, reassuringly.

Anitha obeyed, gulping the glass of water thirstily.

"Tell me, Anitha," the principal once more removed her spectacles. Her ocean-blue eyes stared at the tear-drenched girl before her. "Tell me, why do you think the girls hate you?"

Anitha blinked away her tears, furiously. Her chin raised in regal defiance. Salted tears stung her raw wounds. "They hate me because I am intelligent."

Mrs Halliwell tilted her fair head to one side. "That's my girl," she whispered, smiling.

CHAPTER SEVEN

York Minster with its grey stones loomed large and bleak as mother and daughter walked wordlessly on the cobbled streets of The Shambles. Sore from being suspended from school, Anitha almost blindly knocked into the black and white board that advertised the daily Ghost Walk.

She shuddered as always when she had to pass this way although with time and practice, she learned to mute the screams of the beheaded and blur the vivid images of blood and flies and rolling heads from centuries before.

"Shall we attend the evensong at five?" Durga suggested.

It had been two days since Anitha's suspension. She had thrown herself into her geography project and retreated into monumental sulky moods that stretched for hours in a day. Anitha shrugged her shoulders. She didn't care to answer.

"It's your birthday tomorrow. Shall we eat at El Piano's?" Durga attempted to sound upbeat.

Anitha loved eating at El Piano's. The restaurant served a variety of cosmopolitan vegan food and drink. The place itself was beautiful with its artistic décor of the exotic and quirky.

"Whatever…" Anitha stopped to stare into the red-framed window of Tulliver's, a whole food and complementary medicine shop. She scanned the range of gluten-free biscuits. "Can I have one?"

"Sure."

The bell clanged as they entered the shop. Anitha browsed as her mother dropped the boxes of biscuits into a basket. She searched the shelf of teas and picked out a tin of lemon and ginger tea.

"Hey you…"

It was him.

For the second time in her life, Anitha's brain took a dip. Her palms began to sweat. She opened her mouth to say hello.

It stayed open.

"Remember me?"

How could one forget an encounter with a Norse God? His lopsided grin set against glimmering green eyes made her knees wobbly.

"Who's this?" Durga stood beside her daughter armed with a basketful of biscuits, herb teas and two bottles of Bach's "Five Flower Rescue Remedy".

Solomon held out his hand. "I'm Solomon," he confidently introduced himself.

"I'm Anitha's mother." Durga shook the boy's hand.

"Is that her name?" Solomon teased. His brows crinkled.

"Have the two of you met before?" Durga quizzed. Heat rose in Anitha's cheeks.

"Last week my cat found its way into your home. I came by to deliver some pamphlets…"

Anitha closed her mouth.

"What sort of pamphlets?"

"Well, ma'm, during spring and summer break, I do odd jobs around the garden…for a small sum… negotiable…"

"Do you have a pamphlet with you now?"

Solomon whipped out a couple of pieces of paper from his haversack.

Durga read it, interestedly. "I could do with some assistance…but no promises." She folded the paper and slipped it into her handbag.

Anitha studied the floor earnestly as life passed by with each beat of her heart.

"Thank you, m'am. As I said, the fee is negotiable." He sounded all grown-up.

Too cute…

"It's my birthday tomorrow!" Anitha blurted.

The shop blurred in front of her.

A whirring ring echoed in her ears.

She could not breathe.

The tin of tea in her hand clattered onto the floor.

Solomon bent to pick up the tea. "Happy Birthday, Anitha," he chuckled as he handed the tin to her mother.

CHAPTER EIGHT

By the banks of the river, she sat beneath weeping willows. It was a windless, moonless night. Her toes were dipped in the cool, silver waters. She was not afraid. The sensation to slip in was tempting. Her limbs tingled. Ripples tickled her toes.

In she went.

The waters enveloped her, their wetness clinging to her like skin.

She breathed.

Her legs glided.

Her eyes were open, unblinking.

Jewel-encrusted buildings of finest architecture shimmered radiantly before her. Curious, she swam into one dome-shaped structure flanked by winged serpents carved from marble and sparkling precious stones. Easily, she swam through the arched doors rising above 20 feet high.

Inside, there were shelves, hundreds, thousands, no, an infinite number of shelves lined with books, scrolls and state-of-the-art computers and other forms of reading and writing materials never seen by her before. There were no lights as she knew lights to be but the interior was illuminated with a brightness that was unearthly. Her fingers traced through the spines of the books as she floated gracefully from shelf to shelf.

Whispers and chanting washed through her.

Talismanic inscriptions blinked on and off in mid space.

Numbers and mathematical formulations flashed across her mind.

Illegible words from a time before time scribbled themselves upon her forehead.

It was all too much.

A seizure overcame her.

She lurched backwards.

Terrified, her feet kicked in all directions. Her arms flailed helplessly. Water rushed into her mouth. She was drowning!

A hand, old and familiar, suddenly clasped her, pulling her upwards, upwards towards the surface of the river. Her head bobbed. Willow trees swayed in greeting with their solemn prostration. Rays of sunshine plunging into the waters steadied her nerves.

The hand was still holding her.

It felt reassuring.

It was not going to leave her to die.

A wind blew.

Happy Birthday, Anitha, the leaves upon the willows rustled.

The fragrance of garlic-infused scrambled eggs welcomed Anitha as she walked down the stairs. She stopped by the dining room doorway. On the table lay a small basket. In it were bundles of lavender and rosemary stems and a bouquet of wild flowers tied with a yellow ribbon. A small card was attached to the side.

"It was outside by the porch this morning when I opened the door. He must have left it there before going to school." Emerging from the kitchen, Durga placed two plates of scrambled eggs and a bowl of mixed-berry granola oats on the table.

"Who?" Dazed from the near-death dream, Anitha lingered awhile before picking a stem of lavender and smelling it. It smelled beautiful. Peaceful.

"Solomon, of course…" Durga ground some coarse black pepper into the eggs.

Anitha's mind whizzed into a dizzy spell. She needed to sit.

"Sweet sixteen, princess." Durga hugged her daughter, kissing her on her cheeks.

Swallowing a gulp, Anitha wrapped her arms

around her mother's neck. "Oh, ma!"

Durga poured a cup of almond milk into the bowl of oats. "Eat."

Hungry, Anitha attacked her peppery eggs first. There was a hint of pink rose petals in them. After a few mouthfuls, Anitha picked up the card. It simply read, "Happy Birthday." Her heart skipped speedily, merrily. Her spirit rose. She could almost feel wings sprouting from her back. She was ready to take flight…

"I've never seen you so excited about another human being before…" chimed in Durga.

Embarrassed, Anitha decided to pay attention to her oats.

The telephone rang. Durga put her fork down and went to the living room to answer the call. "It's for you! It's grandpa!" she raised her voice.

Anitha stopped eating to pick up the telephone. "Hi, grandpa," her tone quivered. She loved the old man despite not spending time with him. He was always sweet and kind with his words. Besides, he was proud of her academic success and intelligence. He said so. In every conversation. Without fail.

"Happy Birthday, Beti," he wished her, his voice feeble and raspy from cancer. "I love you and I am proud of you."

"Thank you, grandpa." Anitha was on the verge of tears as she remembered the skeletal form of her grandpa at Chandra's wedding. They had exchanged affectionate glances and he even managed to sneak in blowing a kiss.

"Study hard, Beti and I will visit you in Cambridge."

"You promise?" Tears flooded Anitha's eyes.

"For you, anything, Beti..."

"I love you, grandpa..."

"I love you too. You are the smartest person I know. I am proud of you."

"Grandpa?"

"Yes, Beti?"

Anitha stammered. "I...I am sorry..."

"What for?"

"The wedding..."

"Oh that...my daughter deserved the slap."

"No...no grandpa...I...I strangled Uma...in the... in the loo..."

It was quiet on the other line.

"Grandpa?"

"And why did you do that?"

"She called mum an awful name...and she...she said...I was a curse...I killed..." Anitha could not continue. She was trying to muffle her sobs.

"Beti, don't cry. It is over."

Anitha wiped her tears. "I love you, grandpa..."

"Move forward with your life," he advised. "I love you too."

Once more, there was a lull. Anitha waited for her grandfather to put the telephone down.

"Beti," he started.

"Yes?"

"Be careful…" he warned, sagely. Click.

CHAPTER NINE

A squirrel leapt in front of them on the path before scurrying up a birch tree. Durga flung a handful of nuts on the grass. Hurriedly, the creature rushed down, grabbed its bounty and made its way up the tree again.

The day was cloudy with a slight chill breeze. Anitha and Durga had planned on this walk along the Pennine trail, minutes from their home in the Ferry Close. The countryside with its expansive, green fields of wheat, barley and beets arched by the blue grey skies soothed her nerves.

Be careful...

Grandpa's words rung eerily in her ears.

A great tit with its black head, white cheek patches and yellow underbelly hopped alongside them, pecking the ground. Durga scattered a generous mix of seeds and raisins. Moments later, a couple of blackbirds and a lone robin joined the banquet. The pair resumed their walk, occasionally giving way to cyclists.

"You were right," Durga started.

"Huh?" Anitha's mind was still fogged by her conversation with her granddad.

"We should have never gone to the wedding but I felt you needed to connect with your cousins, you know, being a single child and all. Children your age have cousins to hang around with and aunts and uncles to dote on them. You have nobody except me...I feel it's not enough..."

"I don't need family like that, mum. Life is peaceful without them. Sometimes, yes, it gets lonely but that is a better option than being with them. Don't let your guilt ruin what we have, mum – peace and quiet. I am not one of those teenagers who have a desperate need to belong..."

Durga did not respond immediately. "Since when did you grow up so quickly?" she mused with pride.

"Since forever..."

The rest of the day sailed smoothly. After a delicious lunch of butter bean and vegetable soup with tortilla chips and spicy salsa at El Piano's, Durga and Anitha strolled around the Museum Gardens, admiring the kaleidoscope of summer blooms before deciding to rest on the mowed lawns.

The ruins of St Mary's Abbey lent a solemn air to an otherwise predictable summer cheer. The chatter of tourists and constant clicks of cameras buzzed around. Tourist guides led groups on the York walks. Many, stretched on mats, were enjoying a late-afternoon snooze. Families with their picnics made temporary abodes on select sites. Children ran around, screeching and playing, their eyes shining, skins slick with sweat. Long queues stretched from the ice cream van. The atmosphere was one of leisure and laziness.

"I was thinking," Durga unrolled a vegan chocolate cake from her tissue wrap.

Anitha was watching a peacock butterfly perch on a chosen pink buddleia.

"I was thinking we should visit your grandmother during the summer break..."

Anitha forgot she had another grandparent. A bee flew past her to enter into the nearby patch of foxgloves. "You mean, your mother...?"

"Of course, silly..."

"The one in Kerala?"

Durga nodded.

Anitha bit into the cake.

"Well?"

"I don't know her." That was the truth, Anitha figured.

"She is your grandmother."

"Why now?" Anitha asked, cautiously.

"It is time…"

Eyeing her mother warily, Anitha was stunned by the strange, golden shimmering in her eyes. It was as if they were not her mother's eyes. They belonged elsewhere.

A baby wailed.

A cocker spaniel galloped to and fro, its tongue lolling happily as someone threw him a stick.

A father scolded his child for spilling ice cream.

The air began to slide in a glinting ripple. Dusty, ghostly echoes of sombre chants coming from the ruins of the abbey haunted Anitha. Grainy images of Benedictine nuns flashed in her mind's eye, their veiled figures with heads hung low in reverence, weaving their shadows through long, dim corridors.

"It is time, you know…" Durga whispered.

CHAPTER TEN

It was a perfect summer's afternoon, well, according to Anitha anyway. She was back in school, the research on her fracking project was moving along swiftly, and here she was with Solomon beneath the embracing glow of the sun as it washed itself over the willowed Ouse.

They were seated on the garden chairs facing the pleasure cruises going past. A family of swans bobbed with each sweeping wave. At first, Anitha had been surprised that her mother had invited Solomon for a late afternoon meal but Durga assured her that it was purely for business. She needed to discuss garden maintenance during summer break with Solomon.

Ebony laid on the lawn, her furry, black body rising and falling with each sleeping breath.

"She was my mother's..." Solomon sighed.

Anitha kept watching the cat.

"She stopped looking after her. Her episodes were too frequent and violent. One day, I was back from school and I found her strangling the cat."

Anitha stiffened.

"I pulled Ebony away. She then tried to strangle me. I hit her and then called the police." Solomon took a swig of his lemonade. "My grandparents take me to London to visit her every month."

"She's alive?" Anitha shrunk at her own reaction.

"Well, of course she is! She's not dead! She's just locked up."

"Then why do you refer to her in the past tense?!" Anitha sounded annoyed.

"She's not the mother I remember when I was much younger. She was gentle and loving. A few years ago, she was diagnosed with schizophrenia. I don't know how that happens but it does. Apparently, the condition can remain dormant till adulthood."

"And your dad?"

"He left. My mother's parents care for me now. I moved up North here last year to be with them. I go to St Joseph's, just round the corner from St Anne's."

A hover fly landed on Ebony's tail. Anitha watched it groom itself.

"And you?" Solomon asked.

"Huh?"

"What happened to your dad?"

"He's not here."

"Right." Solomon poured a jug of lemonade into his glass. "Why not?"

"Car crash. I was three months old. I survived."

She heard the crush of metal.

The wail of a baby.

The smell of blood clung thickly in the air.

"Anitha!" was his last word.

She remembered.

"Anitha!"

With a blink and a jump, Anitha felt her body fall off the chair. Solomon helped her up.

"Whoa!" he exclaimed as he returned to his seat. "What happened there?"

Her mind still hazy from the graphic images and the deafening sounds, Anitha shook her head.

"You didn't seem to hear me. Your eyes went all funny like they were fluttering. Then you just fell off your chair!"

A voice called out from inside the house. "Time to eat!"

Anitha mumbled an apology. This was way too embarrassing. She was relieved when the food arrived. It was a brilliant distraction.

There was mixed roast vegetables seasoned with garlic, olive oil and coarse black pepper. A bowl of steaming brown rice sat by the side of the vegetable platter. Durga had also whipped up a traditional South Indian salad, raita – chopped cucumber with yoghurt, mint and sea salt.

"Whoa!" Solomon widened his eyes as he reached out for a poppodum. "This looks delicious!"

"Please help yourself," Durga smiled, pleased with the reaction.

Solomon piled the sliced aubergines, yellow and green peppers and okra on his plate. Durga scooped some rice and placed it next to the vegetables.

Anitha felt the fire in her belly sparkle. For the first time in her life, she felt…normal…relaxed….she watched her mother and Solomon eat and talk and laugh and discuss the gardening that needed to be done when she and her mother would be away in Kerala.

Kerala.

Her mother's mother…

What did mum mean when she said "it is time you know"?

"Oh my God!" It was Solomon. He was staring down at her hands.

Anitha and Durga followed his eyes.

There, sitting on her left hand was a beetle of iridescent greenish hue.

"It's a Tansy beetle!" Solomon exclaimed excitedly. "Do you know how rare it is? It is a species of SSI…"

There was no comment. The two before him appeared clueless.

"The Tansy beetle is of Special Scientific Interest. It can only be found around the Ouse in York. Nowhere else! There are only approximately 500 of them recorded to survive. Most live at Rawcliffe Meadows. Wow! Fancy one on your hand!"

Anitha felt heat rising in her cheeks. She gazed down at her hand. The beautiful beetle gleamed a deep, greenish gold in the sun. It seemed to be at home on her still hand. It must have crawled from somewhere down the river bank and into the garden.

Ebony, with her yellow slant of eyes, was studying Anitha. Her tail flicked.

Suddenly, the skin on her hand shifted.

The beetle moved slightly.

Her skin, like a soft carpet, undulated. There was movement beneath her skin.

The beetle edged away from the centre of her hand.

Ebony watched with knowing intent.

Anitha's heartbeat hit hard against her chest. Watery mists veiled her eyes. Her limbs slipped and slid from their joints or so she thought. Something was moving inside of her.

Underneath her skin.

Noises faded in the background. The rays of the sun clouded in her mind. Only the green body of the

Tansy beetle appeared vivid like a rare jewel. Through blurred vision, she squinted. Her brown skin and the Tansy green merged and mingled, dancing amid shadows and speckled sunbeams. A scream struggled in her throat.

There was the clatter of chairs and raised voices. Darkness fell.

CHAPTER ELEVEN

Anitha was inconsolable.

She wept the entire week. Even when she trudged to school, she cried inside her heart.

Solomon never dropped by again. There was not even a telephone call. Durga had to make urgent calls to several gardeners who could be available to tend to the garden during the summer break. They never spoke of the incident that spooked Solomon days ago.

Anitha knew.

She saw him see her skin change…

Her dreams during sleep time were now dangerously intruding upon her waking hours. They were becoming almost real. Literally, before her eyes, she had witnessed and felt her skin change…change into something she could not understand. Something in her mother's eyes though told otherwise. Her mother was privy to some sort of knowledge that was kept from Anitha.

This angered Anitha.

So mother and daughter stopped addressing each other except for basic reasons – meals and school. Durga busied herself with travel plans and shopping and packing while Anitha occupied herself with weeping and schoolwork.

And touching and observing her skin…

It was the last day of school. Anitha dragged her feet across the streets and the village park, which was now bursting with the colours of summer's best blooms. Oak trees provided cool shade beneath the warming sun. Several yew trees lined the edge of the park. Some were evidently more than a thousand years old. Yews were Anitha's favourite trees. She glanced at her watch. She was still early for school. Walking towards the nearest yew tree, she put down her bag and sat on a coil of gnarled roots – old, cracked and splitting. This one was old, very, very old. With a sinking, sad heart, her fingers traced the roughness and unevenness of the meandering roots. Strangely, it comforted her.

An unspeakable silence entered her.

It stilled her agitated spirit.

Even the traffic and the birds fell quiet.

"Well, well, well, what do we have here?" someone snorted derisively. It was Chloe, the ringleader, twirling her blonde ponytail with her forefinger. Beside her posed her two squad members, Betty and Fiona with arms akimbo. Three pairs of cold, blue eyes sized her up and down.

"Teacher's pet…" Fiona kicked Anitha's schoolbag, laughing throatily.

As Anitha tried to reach out to grab her bag, Betty shoved her to the ground while Chloe pressed her foot down on Anitha's chest. Helplessly, Anitha watched Fiona dancing and skipping as she scattered the contents of her bag across the lawn.

"You got us suspended…" snarled Chloe close to Anitha's ears.

"You think you are so smart? Smarter than the rest of us?" Fiona slapped Anitha on the right cheek. Betty snatched a clump of hair from Anitha's head and yanked it.

Anitha let out an agonising yell. "Why are you doing this to me?" her voice wobbled tearfully. Her fingers clung desperately to the entwining roots of the yew tree.

"We don't like your face or your attitude," smirked Chloe as she dangled a file labelled 'Anahitha.' "This must be your geography project. Hmmm…"

"Give it back!" screamed Anitha, her throat, dust dry.

"Give it back!" mocked Fiona in a singsong fashion.

"Give it back! Give it back! Give it back!" the threesome taunted in unison.

Chloe took a deep breath as she bowed theatrically and in slow motion began to tear the first page of the fracking project.

Anitha froze.

Her body shuddered.

Her mind fogged with watery mists swirling in front of her eyes.

A low hissing hum thrummed against her body as she hunched on all fours.

She looked down on her skin. It was shifting in wave-like motions, filtering a variety of hues. Her blood flowed hot and cold at the same time. A feverish chill slithered through her. She closed her eyes as it burned not fire but ice.

The sensation was tranquillising.

She was falling asleep.

Something else inside her was waking up.

A feline growl shattered her spell. Her eyes shot open. She saw Ebony in mid-leap as the cat landed neatly on Chloe, clawing her cheeks with a single swipe. Crablike, Chloe stumbled backwards, her arms shielding her face from further attacks. Fiona and Betty were already running away from the scene.

Anitha flashed her eyes at Chloe. Suddenly, she saw everything clearly…very, very clearly: the intense colours, the throbbing veins, the flow of blood through limbs, the pump of the heart…she heard the beat as loud as though it was her own…she smelled the fear before her…

Chloe sprang to her feet, her face as white as death, as though she had just encountered a ghost. She could not scream. Her words were garbled as she pointed at Anitha's eyes before collapsing into a faint.

"Ebony!"

The black cat flicked its tail, refusing to heed the call. It moved towards Anitha, licking her hands.

"Ebony!" Solomon ran towards Chloe. A crowd was gathering. Someone had called the police. He faced Anitha.

His eyes said it all.

The girl before him was a monster.

CHAPTER TWELVE

The stone well was round in the middle of an empty space.
She peered in. The water was clear and still. Her reflection
stared back at her.

Her eyes.

Vertical slits against a yellowish hue.

Anitha's eyes flew open. Her palms were sweaty. Her
body was shaking. Something was happening to her
and she was horrified. Once again, her blood boiled
with anger. She heard the bell ringing and her mother
chanting.

It was Saturday morning.

Puja day.

Friday was over.

She remembered grabbing her bag and dashing off
to school leaving Solomon at the scene of the incident.

She remembered her skin returning to normal and her eyes regaining usual vision. Back in class, nobody called for her. No police. No Mrs Halliwell. No mother. Nobody. The last day at school was rather undramatic.

Solomon had called her mother later in the evening recounting the entire episode. Apparently, when paramedics arrived, Chloe could not remember anything. She did not know why she was there in the park in the first place. She was still under suspension along with Fiona and Betty. Fiona and Betty had said nothing. They weren't about to confess to bullying. Besides, they did not witness anything. Only Chloe and Solomon saw what had happened to her...and thankfully, Chloe had no memory of her trauma.

Solomon.

Anitha trusted Solomon.

He would not tell. He could not.

Anitha charged downstairs. Durga had just entered the dining room with her bell and incense. Dawn was setting a golden glow in the space.

"Tell me the truth! Mum! What is happening to me!"

Durga paused, her back to her daughter.

"Who are we?! No! What are we?!"

There was no response.

"Do I have a disease? Am I sick?!"

Durga put down the bell and the incense on the dining table. "You do not have a disease and you are not sick." Her back was still to Anitha. "It is who you are. It is who we are."

The birds outside chirped.

"And what is that, mum? A monster? Is that who I am? A monster…is that who you are?"

Durga turned, her face suddenly worn and haggard. "No. Just different."

"Stop with the riddles and codes. I need facts. Pure, simple facts." Anitha bit her lips. She wanted to hit her mother.

"I am tired. Tomorrow we leave for Kerala. You will meet your grandmother. You will know…" Durga went to the kitchen and put the kettle on for tea.

"You are my mother! You tell me!" Anitha flung a mug across the kitchen. It crashed into smithereens.

It was quiet save for the tick tock of the kitchen clock.

"It's always about you isn't it, Anitha?!" Durga banged her fists on the counter top.

"What?" Anitha was bewildered.

"It's always been about bloody you…your pain, your sadness, your loneliness…"

"What?" Anitha stepped back.

Her mother faced her squarely with clenched hands.

"What about my pain…my guilt? I am sick of

protecting you and your feelings! I am tired of this mothering crap!" Durga mewled, her arms embracing her rocking body. "All I wanted was Amit…just Amit and me…happily ever after…just Amit and me…I miss him…I miss him…ohhhh…" a keening moan lingered in the air.

"Mum, what are you saying?"

"When I told Amit…he wanted me to keep you… he didn't know about me…I was in love…and terrified if he ever found out, he would leave me…and here you are…" Durga mocked a laugh. "…and he's gone…"

A rush of hot tears drenched Anitha. She could not believe her mother was saying this. Her body broke into chills. It was happening again…the changing… no…she dared not look at her skin but she felt the movement weaving through her limbs. "I hate you!" Anitha spat out. "I hate you!"

Durga burst into a fit of delirious giggles. Tears streamed down her quivering cheeks.

"I really hate you!"

Durga crumpled to the floor, bent over, crying and laughing at the same time. "Whatever…" she said before curling herself into a foetal position,

sobbing and gasping like a sickly newborn baby.

Kerala

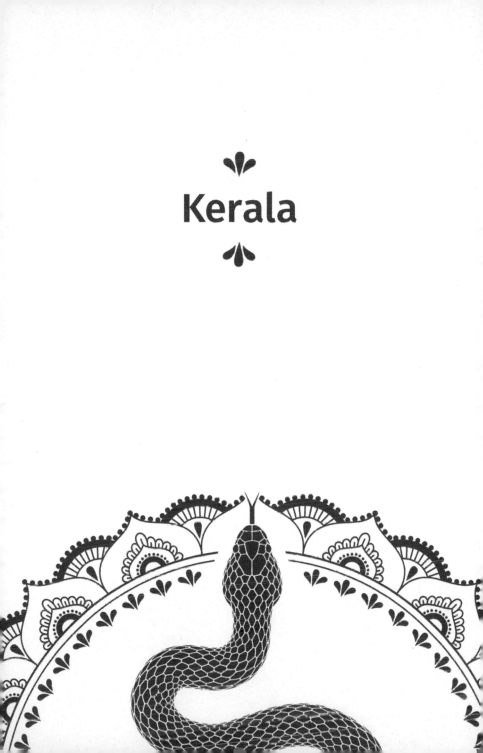

CHAPTER THIRTEEN

As the plane geared for landing, Anitha inclined her head against the window. The deep, clear blue of the waters of the Western Ghats set against the green of the lined palm trees swaying in the sea breeze, meandering through small fishing villages and their lazy rivers comforted Anitha considerably.

She glanced at the woman beside her, asleep and lost in a space that Anitha was not welcome to. Her mother had slept on the kitchen floor till lunchtime. Neither spoke a word till the next day. They left for the airport silently and, throughout the entire trip, Durga had opted to close her eyes and disappear into her own world. Even when it was time to eat, the air steward was met with a grim 'do not disturb' expression.

After the hassle at the immigration checkpoint, a

five-foot young man greeted them outside the airport with a huge grin. He rushed to grab their luggage and pile it in the boot of the car. Grandmother had requested a driver to pick them up and drop them off at her home. Anitha was grateful. The heat and humidity was oppressive. Sweat clung to her like a second skin. The chatter of loud conversations in Malayalam around her felt overwhelming.

"Thank you," she smiled kindly.

"You're most welcome, madam," came the cheerful response. He spoke English with a slight lilting accent.

Stone-faced, Durga crawled into the back seat.

Slightly embarrassed, Anitha apologetically offered a small smile to the man and allowed herself to sit at the front.

"So this is your first time?" he started, his face still bearing the most endearing grin.

He must be in his thirties, Anitha estimated. His eyes were large and honest, his features, typically small and delicate. "Yes." She peered out the window.

The streets were relatively clean and thrumming with people on their daily routines. Small stalls with bright advertisement boards were alive with local fast foods and traditional drinks. Despite the constant honk of vehicles and flying dusts of sand, people were seated outside on wooden benches enjoying hearty meals of flat bread and spiced hot gravy.

"Do you know my grandmother?" Anitha asked, curiously.

The driver paused for a cow taking its time to cross the road. "Of course. I work for your grandmother."

"You're her driver?"

"I drive her around, I shop for her groceries and I help out with the garden, and my wife cleans her home. She pays well and she is good to my children."

She sounds nice enough, thought Anitha. "Does she have many friends? What about family? Relatives who come around for visits?" Anitha wondered if she had extended family...

The man laughed. "She prefers her own company most of the time unless she is called for a cause..."

"Oh?"

"You don't know much about her do you?"

Nothing, Anitha wanted to say but refrained.

"She's quite the controversy..." he left it at that.

The car turned away from the main street. Now, they were on a quiet, darker lane flanked by long, lean groves of coconut trees. Nobody walked this way, Anitha sensed. She heard the murmur of rivers. Soon, the car slowed to a driveway. A single-storey white house with a spacious porch stood solitary surrounded by a lush tropical garden. Anitha spotted a mango tree laden with the golden fruits. A peahen strutted past the car. It made Anitha giggle.

The driver was already unloading the suitcases and carrying them to the front door. Anitha stepped out of the car. The place smelled fresh and clean. There was the hint of sea in the air. "Thank you," she said as the driver returned to take one more bag. "I'm Anitha…"

"I'm Kumar…"

Durga opened the car door, trudging her way to the porch. Into the house she went without a word.

"And that's my mother," Anitha sighed.

CHAPTER FOURTEEN

The Grandmother summoned her.

Anitha had taken a shower, changed and tucked into crispy cauliflower and pea samosas when she was called for.

The room was grandmother's study. It had a library filled with books, a large, rectangular work-table with a laptop, a printer, files of papers and notes. There was a long window that overlooked another part of the garden. Anitha could see a rivulet hidden cosily amongst the dark green of the plants and trees.

"Come here, child…" the voice was solid and firm.

Obediently, Anitha stepped forward. The woman on the armchair was barely five-foot, dark-brown complexioned with perfectly refined doll-like features. A smoothly combed, ballerina bun stood neatly on her head. Everything about her was small and fragile but

Anitha felt in her guts that the woman was far from cute and needy.

"My mother…where is she?" Anitha asked. No matter what had taken place between her and her mother, she still cared for her. She was her mother. The only family Anitha had ever known…

The Grandmother took a sip from her hot tea. "Your mother is resting. She needs to rest. She will not be disturbed."

"When will I see her?" Anitha sounded frightened. The old, beautiful woman was unnerving.

"Anitha, your mother just suffered a nervous breakdown."

The ground beneath Anitha felt loose and slippery. "Wh…what does that mean?"

"It means her mind, body and spirit are exhausted and she needs rest before she is able to return to caring for you."

Anitha's mind started spinning. Her heart pounded fearfully. Here she was in a strange country with a strange, old woman called grandmother and no mother to look out for her. She swallowed a tearful choke.

"Will she get better?"

The Grandmother smiled. It was soft and sad at the same time. "She should."

"This is not exactly a holiday, is it?"

Grandmother gave a little laugh and shook her

head. "No, it is not."

"Why am I here?" Anitha was not sure if she wanted to know the truth. She knew she just wanted to pack her bags and take the next flight back to York where summer beckoned her. Suddenly, she missed her room, her routines and the long walks down the riverbank and on the Pennine trail. She longed to watch her birds feed on the nuts and seeds…

"This visit is long overdue, Anitha. I was expecting you some years back but one can't force nature's cycle."

Anitha stared, wide-eyed and confused.

"Sit, child and let me explain."

Anitha sat on the long couch that faced the window. She pulled a cushion to her lap.

"I am aware of what you are going through and you want an explanation."

Anitha shivered.

"You are going through what we call The Changing…I call it The Shedding…Anitha, my dear, surely by now you must know you are different… different from others…"

"How…how do you…about the skin…changing…? And who is 'we'?"

"Your mother and I are in constant communication. We were expecting this to occur when you were between ten to thirteen years of age when girls normally attain puberty but you took a little longer, didn't you, child?"

Anitha cringed. It was true. She had her first period only three months ago.

"And 'we' are you and me and your mother and those like us…" The Grandmother allowed herself a pause and a sip of her late afternoon tea. Then, she rose slowly from her chair and walked towards Anitha.

She knelt, clutched Anitha's hands lightly and whispered, "You, Anitha, you are your Mother's daughter. You are of Serpent Born."

The walls shimmered into a watery haze. Her limbs moved freely with the waters. There were others like her swimming around her. Their scales shone in a range of colours. Their hoods nodded at her. Slender tails flicked in friendly greeting. She recognised two of them although they did not look like they should but she knew in her heart that they were them…her mother, her grandmother…

"Wake up!"

She woke up. "Who are…you?" Old, brown eyes watched her as she revived from her unconsciousness. "Who…am…am…I?"

The Grandmother stroked her hair. "I am your grandmother. Your mother is your mother and you are you…of Serpent Born. Dear Anitha, I need you to listen. I ask you not to faint on me or get emotional or hysterical. It will not help. Whether you like it or not, you must and will know. It is wise, child, to pay attention."

Anitha pondered on her life.

The death of her father, being raised by mum, going through life with no friends and extended family, the torment, the bullying…the loneliness, the ache in the heart…Solomon…Anitha wiped the tears from her eyes, sat up straight and said, "Right…I am ready, Grandma. Tell me. I am listening."

CHAPTER FIFTEEN

Grandmother began, "We are, Anitha, a race of beings unique in our DNA…like every creation…humans, animals, plants. The cosmos is infinitely bigger than what we know it to be. This understanding surpasses human limitations. Human history is proof that what humans cannot see or measure or explain away is demonised, reviled or simply misunderstood.

Our DNA is specifically serpentine.

Here in the subcontinent, we are referred to as the Nagas. It is the presence of our bloodline that authenticates the royal lineage of humans.

We exist and vibrate on a separate frequency from the human realm. There are other unique beings existing on separate vibrations, terrestrial and non-terrestrial. It is like tuning into different radio frequencies. Just because you prefer listening to pop music and feel its energy and beat does not mean that the other channels are not playing their own music at the same time. It simply means you are not tuned into those other frequencies.

Let me give you another example. Electricity. Can you see electricity?"

Anitha said no. Her fears and hysterics had suddenly vanished. Instead, she latched onto every word spoken by this grandmother woman before her.

"Just because you can't see electricity does it mean it is not there?"

Again, Anitha muttered a fascinated no.

"Can you see air?"

"No. I cannot." Anitha's eyes gleamed curiously.

"Does it mean it doesn't exist?"

"No."

"Yet, we use electricity and we breathe air to survive. It is the same with us…our kind. Just because humans can't generally see us does not deny our existence. As a matter of fact, we were here long before them…" the grandmother woman gave a smug smile.

Anitha smiled too although she did not know why she smiled along with her.

"Now comes the interesting bit…listen." The Grandmother sat herself beside Anitha. Anitha huddled closer. It felt safe. The Grandmother smelt of spice and herbs. Her voice transformed into a secret whisper.

"In many ancient spiritual traditions, we occupied an important place in human ritual and worship. Humans approached us because of our semi-divine status. Offerings were presented to us in exchange for answered prayers. Our kind had access to knowledge and power that humans needed or desired."

"What did humans pray to the nagas for?" Anitha asked. The word semi-divine had made her skin tingle.

"The usual – wealth, health, babies, jobs, love… just about anything. Of course, depending on each individual & not all prayers are answered easily. That is just the way life plays out."

"Oh…" Anitha mumbled disappointedly. She was thinking of Solomon. Her heart cracked. She heard it.

Did this grandmother person hear it too?

"Of course it was not just prayers and offerings that we required from humans to sustain the relationship. It was deeper than that. It was vital that humans cared for the land upon which they lived – the air, the soil and particularly in our case, the waters of this planet. For we, Anitha, are basically water beings. Water is our lifeline. It is the channel through which our DNA perpetuates generation after generation. You poison water. You poison life."

Anitha sat up. Her fracking project came to her mind. She sensed a feeling that suddenly nothing was a coincidence.

"Once upon a time," the Grandmother continued sadly, "there was respect and a symbiotic working relationship between humans and us." She stroked her hair, tucking a few strands to the back of her left ear. "Now, we are the stuff of legends, superstitions and objects of disgust and fear."

"How did that happen?" Anitha recalled Solomon's reaction to her changing. Shame peppered her mixed emotions.

"There are many reasons, one of them being the presence of rogue elements in both societies. You see, Anitha, all beings are gifted with opportunities to evolve within themselves. However, some choose to sacrifice this soul evolution for instant satisfaction whether it is material, emotional or mental. "

"So how do we help our souls to be...uh...better?"

The grandmother cupped Anitha's cheeks in her hands. Her golden, brown eyes shone like finely-cut jewels. Mesmerised, Anitha returned the gaze. Her own eyes received the heat of the grandmother's soft warm glow.

"Love...child..." the grandmother declared... fiercely, passionately. "Love...love everything...love all...even the wicked...just love..."

CHAPTER SIXTEEN

All night, Anitha fumed. She refused to sleep. She could not. While the crickets outside interrupted the otherwise silent night, hate filled inside of her.

She hated Chloe, Betty and Fiona for making school hell for her. She hated her father's family, especially Uma, for being mean towards her mother and her. She hated them for making her feel responsible for her father's...she hated her mother for trying too hard... it was pitiful...she hated Solomon so much because he made her feel ugly and because she loved him in a way she never thought she could love a boy and now she would never be with him...she hated her father for not being with her...she hated not knowing him and never knowing him...and him never knowing her...

Above all, she hated herself...her life...

And if that was not bad enough, she now hated this

grandmother…hated the old woman for telling her to love…how dare she! What did she know!

Anitha's stomach growled hungrily. She was so mad she had skipped dinner that the Grandmother had prepared. She spent the rest of the entire day in her room. It was bad manners but Anitha did not care.

She beat her pillow.

She punched it hard and buried her face into it and ranted and screamed…

…the whole night…

Her head throbbed. The whites of her eyes were a raw pink and her throat stung dry. It was eight in the morning. She opened the curtain to the window. A flood of glaring yellow sunshine charged into the room.

Rubbing her eyes, Anitha peered out into the back garden. It was surprisingly large with several tropical bushes and plants greeting her with their splendid colours on proud display. In the middle was a well made of stone. It was not particularly big but neither was it small. Disused, most probably, Anitha figured. However, there was no overgrown moss nor wild plants creeping amok around the well. It was suspiciously clean and maintained.

A kingfisher spotted her and flapped its pretty wings before disappearing into the lush green darkness of what looked like intricate mazes of freshwater swamps or marshes. She scanned intently. Something caught her eye.

A couple of yards away from the well was a standing stone structure of about three foot. The top fanned outwards like a hood. Beneath this canopy was a long, beautiful black cobra, coiled elegantly, its eyes as radiant as sparkling yellow diamonds. Flowers and leaves were placed in symmetrical patterns around the structure. Sticks of incense inserted in a wooden cup holder were still burning.

Startled, Anitha blinked.

The black cobra was no more.

Wisps of a serpentine trail veiled the stone structure.

A tear slipped down Anitha's left cheek.

Her thoughts were scrambled.

Her feelings were messy.

She was lost.

"Hungry?" The Grandmother did not wait for a reply. Instead she scooped a generous ladle full of steaming lentil and carrot stew into Anitha's bowl. "Help yourself to the dosas. I made them myself this morning." The Grandmother pushed a plate of flatbread made with rice and lentil flour towards Anitha who immediately took one and tore it into pieces before dipping them into the stew. Anitha was ravenous and the breakfast was delicious. "Thank you," she said sullenly, not looking the Grandmother in her eyes. She was still mad. "Where's mum?" she queried, reaching out for a second flatbread. The Grandmother sipped her tea. Anitha could not read her reaction. "Where's mum?" Anitha persisted.

"Resting, child…"

Anitha hunched her shoulders. She had a sad feeling that she was on this trip alone.

Alone and abandoned.

She fought back her tears.

Breakfast proceeded quietly. A petite woman in her twenties with a cheerful face appeared from the kitchen to clear the plates. She was dressed in a plain, cream sari. The Grandmother introduced her. "This is Mira, Kumar's wife. She helps around the house and occasionally does the cooking."

"Nice to meet you, Mira." Anitha nodded at the pretty face with huge, brown eyes and full, pouting lips.

"You too, madam…" replied Mira, shyly.

"Just call me, Anitha…" Anitha lifted her empty bowl to Mira and thanked her "…and just for the record, no one calls me child any more. I am not a child. I am sixteen years old." Anitha faced the Grandmother squarely. She braced herself for a fight. Mira scurried off into the safety of the kitchen.

The Grandmother sipped the last of her tea, rose

from her chair and walked towards the open back door. Pausing, she turned her head, "Well, what are you waiting for…Anitha…? You are not a child any more. It is time to grow up."

CHAPTER SEVENTEEN

Without a word, Anitha got up, put on her slippers and stepped out into the back garden where the Grandmother stood contemplatively beneath a grove of coconut trees.

It was cooler, shadier and definitely more secluded out here than the front garden, Anitha noted, but she was astounded by the diverse growth of flora. She recognised miniature palm trees, pandanus shrubs that exuded a sweet, vanilla-type scent and herb plants of varied kinds.

"Here," the Grandmother offered her a few leaves from a plant beside her.

Anitha rubbed the leaves between her fingers and let the dark, rich earthy aroma sooth her nerves.

"This is Holy Basil; we call it tulsi. It is good in healing fevers, colds, flu but it is also a general tonic for the body and mind that suffers from fatigue. It's a superb anti-depressant."

"It smells gorgeous," admitted Anitha.

"I'll brew a tea with this for you…if you wish…"

Anitha inhaled the leaves again. "Thank you. I'd like that." She strolled further before stopping at a tree with small, oval leaves attached to very thin stems bearing long pods of fruit resembling drumsticks with clusters of small, white, creamy flowers. "I recognise this," she pointed to the pods. "Mum puts them in dhal. I didn't know the tree looked like this!"

"That, my dear, is the moringa tree commonly called drumstick. The west considers it a superfood now. You have the tea versions in your wholefood shops, yes? It contains essential vitamins and minerals. It is an excellent blood cleanser."

Leisurely, Anitha walked, soaking in the intoxicating fragrances and colours of the rest of the garden, which included a red rose bush, jasmine trellises and pink frangipanis. "This is paradise…" she said to the Grandmother, an expression of wonder flushing her face.

"Yes. It is. I do what I can. We do what we can to preserve the sacred and healing natural world."

Anitha paid attention.

"We, Anitha, are guardians and protectors of this natural world we inhabit. Mother Nature is dying.

She dies, we die and all life as we know it dies. It is our duty to be stewards of the earth, not killers. With knowledge, wisdom, education and mindful effort, all life must work in symbiosis to heal the earth…Kerala has been good to us compared to other modern societies of the world. We are still held in reverence here. That is why we are able to thrive as long we have. "

"I understand," Anitha said.

"Anitha, you are of Serpent Born. You are a Naga."

Before the Grandmother could continue, Anitha interjected, "Was my father a Naga?"

"No. He was pure human."

"And mum?"

"She is pure Naga."

"But…but…" Anitha was confused. "But, she, you…I don't get it…look and feel…human…"

"We Nagas are blessed with powers that enable us to enter into human frequencies and appear as flesh and blood humans. Shape-shifting is the best word I can use to describe it. Human frequencies are denser, heavier and highly contaminated. It takes a toll on us. There are those who have lost their lives, physical abilities and those who have had a complete mental breakdown and suffer insanity."

"Like mum? Will…will…she…"

Putting her arms around Anitha's trembling shoulders, the Grandmother assured, "she is well cared for and in a couple of weeks, she's good to go…you stop worrying. My daughter is in expert hands."

A feeling of peace descended upon Anitha. Her heartbeat steadied. "So…if mum is a Naga and dad is human…what does that make me?"

The Grandmother laughed. "Both…technically, you are a hybrid. You have the blood of the Nagas and the human. It is easier for you to travel in both dimensions. There are many hybrids about. Only psychic humans can sense them and those who have attained a certain degree of energy awareness. Other than that, the children of mixed blood prefer not to come out of the closet."

"That's terrible." Anitha's thoughts fled to Solomon.

"Yes. It is too dangerous. Humans are not ready to open their hearts and minds to that which they cannot perceive beyond a three dimensional world view."

Suddenly, there was a hush.

Palm fronds swished in the gentle breeze.

Somewhere nearby, there was the gentle lap of water.

The air was thick with the intermingling of scents.

And a hiss…

Automatically, Anitha clutched the Grandmother's hand…waiting…

"It is time," the Grandmother announced, giving Anitha's hand a cosy squeeze.

"Time? Time for what?"

"It is time for The Shedding."

"The Shedding?"

"You shed your old life and begin anew. Monthly, as a human girl, you shed blood. It is the same as a Naga. You shed skin. It is imperative you take time to shed your skin otherwise your Naga blood will be toxic and you will die.

Do not worry. I will be with you each step of the way. Will you trust me?"

Anitha raised her chin to this grandmother woman. It was as if they had met prior to this visit. "I know you…I know you from somewhere…this is not our first meeting, is it?"

"No."

"You saved me, didn't you…in my dream…I was drowning…you pulled me up from the waters…it was you…it was…"

And the grandmother led her to The Well.

CHAPTER EIGHTEEN

"This is what we, in Kerala here, call the sarpakavu; sarpa for serpent and kavu for shrine," the grandmother explained, pointing to the granite stone structure beside The Well decorated with offerings of incense, flowers and coins. "It is basically a snake shrine dedicated to The Mother. It is common to see many homes and offices around here in towns and villages where a sarpakavu is erected in the southwest corner of the premise."

"The Mother?" Anitha knelt for a closer look. There were nine individual projections resembling fingers that formed the hooded canopy. It was clearly in the shape of a cobra. A yellow butterfly fluttered past, landing on one of the fingers, its wings open to the warm sunshine of the afternoon.

"Yes, The NagaMother...NagaMata, the One who

birthed us all; our kind."

"Oh." Anitha remembered the shadowy cobra from the morning.

"Come, let us begin," the grandmother offered her hand. Anitha received it.

"What do I do?" Anitha saw three steps that led to the top of the well.

"You just need to enter into the well and follow the stepping stones all the way down."

"Why The Well?"

"This particular Well is our Family Well. It is holy. It has been here for a very, very long time. It is The Womb of The Mother. It will take you to one of the backwaters by those coconut groves. Kerala is famous for its backwaters, you know. Tourists come from all over to experience its beauty and peace but don't worry this is private. No boat cruises will be in your way in the water."

Anitha froze. "I can't swim." A wave of terror washed over her as images of her near drowning experience struck her mind in lightning flashes.

She was barely nine and mum and her were picnicking down the riverbank by their home. The day was a glorious summer afternoon. A squirrel had caught her excitement and she had run after it with a sandwich in hand but her foot slipped on the edge of the bank and in she went. The water was cold and she had screamed with her head in the water. It entered her lungs. The pain was excruciating. Her mum and a dog walker had jumped in, rescuing her on time. She was in hospital for about a month. "No. I can't do this. I can't swim." Anitha sucked in the air in shallow, rapid breaths.

"Of course you can swim. I have seen you swim."

"…bu…but…that was in my dreams…" Anitha stared, stunned at the grandmother. "How did…how?"

The grandmother helped her up the three steps. "You were born to swim. The water is your home. It is time to return and be born again."

Anitha peeped down. The steps were scrupulously clean and meandered in a long, winding way downwards. She could not see the bottom of The Well. It was pitch black. However, she could hear the murmur of water.

"I am behind you every step of the way," promised the grandmother. "Remove your slippers."

Anitha removed her slippers and did something that she never imagined she would.

She hugged the grandmother tightly.

"I know. You saved my life."

And Anitha entered The Well.

Her fingers touched the stones of the inside of The Well as she cautiously made her way down. They felt cool and smooth. The air was strangely fresh and light.

The afternoon rays were still lingering lending a glow to the stones that now radiated dark silver hues. Her eyes blinked. The light was lessening. She stopped and turned her head. Grandmother was behind her.

"I am here." Her grandmother's eyes were shimmering like liquid honey. She placed a hand on Anitha'sleft shoulder.

Anitha resumed her journey.

Each step down led Anitha away from the uninterrupted blue of the sky, the gold and warmth of the sunshine, the singsong of birds and the hushing sounds of palm fronds in the wind. Even the heady fragrances of the flowers were fading.

Anitha blinked again. Her lungs expanded with slower, deeper breaths. She felt dizzy, stopping a few seconds before continuing. She was practically feeling her way down. Her eyes soon got used to the darkness as though it had refocused and she could penetrate through the blindness.

Suddenly, her head swam with thoughts, thoughts like intertwining thick coils of mists slithering in the buried recesses of her mind. The vapours of her hidden thoughts choked her. Then her heart thudded as though it had fallen at the end of The Well. Anitha lurched forward but a pair of firm hands encircled and gripped her.

It began...

like a tonne of bricks, it hit her...

...unspoken thoughts, emotions – all intersecting in a single vibrating mass from within each cell of her being, forming peculiar deformed shapes.

She recognised her father inside her - locked up, drowned and dead over and over again in her tears of never-ending grief.

...the guilt she bore for living instead of him...he, so loved by all...

...the sadness for her mother loss and her mother's loneliness...

...the rage against her bullies...

...the panic from the drowning at nine...

...her longing for Solomon...

Thumping her belly with her fists, Anitha howled hysterically, her face, drenched with tears. The echoes bouncing off the stones were deafening. Her knees wobbled, giving way as she leaned against her grandmother for support. They sat on the stepping - stones. Her grandmother stroked her long, black ponytail comforting Anitha with her silence and strength as she listened to her granddaughter weep her life away.

Eventually, fatigued from all the crying, Anitha closed her eyes, laid her head on her grandmother's lap and went to sleep.

CHAPTER NINETEEN

It was her skin that woke her up. It tingled as it fell off in bits and pieces. Her grandmother was still beside her. They were sitting on the stepping-stones.

"How long was I asleep?" Anitha wiped drool off her mouth. Her back ached from the twisted position.

"You needed the sleep."

Anitha witnessed her skin shedding. It was the most natural sensation ever. Pieces of her skin slipped away like autumnal leaves releasing themselves from the clutches of the trees. There was already a small mound of skin on the steps. In its place, she saw the beginnings of tiny scales, glassy and glinting on her arms and legs.

"Do you wish to continue, Anitha? You don't have to. We can always do this tomorrow," her grandmother wiped Anitha's sticky face with a handkerchief. "Here, blow your nose."

Anitha blew her nose till her airways cleared. Her head was light. Some heaviness had been lifted. She breathed easily now. "No, grandma. Another day is another day too long. I have been carrying so much inside me since I was three months old. I need to do this. I want to move on and not be in so much pain all the time. Will you still be with me?"

"I will never leave you out of my sight...hey, did you just call me grandma?"

"You earned it," Anitha giggled, handing back the filthy handkerchief.

"Thank you," her grandmother agreed.

The shedding did not stop. With every downward step, more skin floated weightlessly around her.

The Well was as black and silent as a tomb.

It was the first time in her entire life, Anitha did not hear the noises in her head; the car crash, the crunch of metal, the shatter of glass, her father's groans, him calling out her name...mum's muffled, distressing cries, the bullies with their taunts...

The quiet was so powerful that there was no room for noise.

The blackness was such pure black that she could not see the nightmares that invaded her in her sleep and that plagued her during waking hours.

Suddenly, there was nothing.

Emptiness.

Once again, it was her skin that awakened her.

It bristled with electricity. She gasped, groping her bare self. Her sleeveless shirt and shorts and underwear had all left her. Seeing through the blackness, she spied mounds of skin littering the place.

Stark naked with crystal scales pulsing bright light, she stood in a circular space tiled with stones. Her glossy, scaled feet with toes intact were immersed in cool, clear flowing waters. She gasped at her reflection – her entire self was pure illumination. Her eyes shone a cinnamon gold.

Her grandmother was beside her, still in her crisp, white sari, her breath, warm and steady. "You have been Shed."

"I…I…am so…beautiful." Anitha admired her sudden transformation.

The air hissed.

A shadow uncurled from the waters.

She waited.

The smoky shadow grew and grew till it occupied the height and width of the bottom of The Well. As it expanded, it hissed and hummed. Spellbound, Anitha reached out to touch the greyish vapours.

It enveloped her.

And then there was The Lullaby.

Soft, sweet and melodic.

Unconditional Love.

Dancing in intertwining trails, The Shadow undulated rhythmically, arranging and rearranging in geometric shapes in and around Anitha.

The ground under her feet shifted. Twinkling waters churned in a swirl around her feet. Like a twister, they spiralled upwards to her height before suddenly rushing down her crystal scales like a waterfall.

The Light in The Well struck her blind.

Her grandmother lifted her. Her nerves were scrambled. Her wet, crystal scales vibrated, lightning sparks bounced off the dark walls. Pacing her breath, she leaned against the wall. "Wh...what just ha... happened there?"

"You were cleansed by The Mother."

"The Shadow...that was..."

"The Energy you felt...that was The Mother. The Shadow is how She chose to manifest to you."

"The Shadow...why? Why shadow?"

Her grandmother explained, "The shadow in

general has had a bad press in human history. It has been seen as dark and scary when in fact it is a manifestation of our inner, hidden self that we refuse to see and accept and work with. Humans are experts on duality, separation, this versus that. This world view has been responsible for so much suffering. There is so much we can learn from our individual shadows no matter how painful, disgusting or evil we perceive them to be."

"I don't understand, grandma."

"Within our shadows are lessons we can learn that assist us in our spiritual journey. You, Anitha, have met your shadows. They were physically, mentally and emotionally gruelling but now, at least you can let the light in. There will be many more shadows to come, many more lessons to evolve from. This is life but with love, we ascend…all beings. Love your shadows Anitha and they will take care of you."

"Love…" Anitha repeated. She caressed the scales that now adorned her entire skin. "Grandma?"

"Yes?"

"I…I thought it was going to be a full-on shedding. In my mind, I was turning into a serpent similar to the ones I encountered in my dreams."

"You are half human. This is it."

"Oh."

"You are blessed with the DNA of both worlds."

"Okay. So, what do we do now? Me looking like this?"

"Your dress code is entirely appropriate. My dear, it's time to meet your family."

CHAPTER TWENTY

They walked a few more minutes through a tunnel connected to the bottom of The Well. Russet hues of the sunset sky bathing the lush landscape greeted them. The bubbling river ahead was cosseted among endless groves of marshland, leafy plants and bushes.

Without being urged, Anitha stepped into the waters. Waist deep, she surrendered her body to the river. "Grandma!" she shouted. Grandma was nowhere. "Grandma!" Anitha swam around, closer to the bank. "Grandma!" Something smooth and slippery skimmed past while embracing her in its sturdy coil.

This was grandma.

And grandma was gorgeous. With eyes exquisite as black pearls, she was long and slender, radiating the colours of the brightest sun and the palest silver moon. Embedded in her individual scales were myriads of gemstones that blazed like shooting stars. Her tail was dipped in diamonds galore.

Hello. Talk about bling.

Step aside Kim K...

Together, Anitha and her grandma swam like there was no tomorrow. There was no need to speak with their mouths. Their minds communicated telepathically. Anitha bumped into otters and other river fish before she quickly learned to negotiate her way with the grace and agility of a Naga. Turtles resting on the banks acknowledged her. A family of frogs hopped about, curious about the newest addition to their home. Crabs pinched Anitha the odd time in jest. Pads of rose-pink lotuses exuded a thick perfume each time she swam around them. Water lilies brushed her scales in conscious contact.

Anitha could not believe the variety of aquatic plants and creatures that thrived in her grandmother's private backwater. Each of her super-naga senses absorbed the drumbeat of every cell that lived in this natural, sacred habitat.

Everything was alive and buzzing.

She heard a familiar voice in her mind. It was grandmother, cautioning her to slow down. There was a shimmering, chiming space in front of them. It was like a moving glass wall without a frame. Its frequency was supernaturally high and light, more in tune with her naga-alignment but deaf to her human side.

Side by side, Anitha and her grandmother swam. The force was almost impenetrable for Anitha as her human, denser cells faced the most resistance.

"Relax, don't fight it. Don't bulldoze yourself into the energy. It has been ritually spelled," her grandmother spoke in her head. "Let its frequency calm you. Go with the flow."

Anitha obeyed.

And the flow slipped into her...

"Welcome to the other side."

Feeling disoriented and depleted of energy, Anitha sunk to the riverbed. She was still breathing through her crystal scales. Her human limbs were crooked, disjointed. Her body ached. Pinging rings echoed in her ears.

A team of Nagas, uniquely beautiful, welcomed her, encircling their bodies around each of her limbs, applying pressure that brought about soothing relief as they readjusted her human body. She stirred. Love poured out through each of them into her.

Charged, she was able to swim again.

Awestruck, she saw what she had seen in her dreams: the palaces; pyramids; temples; libraries and family-naga groves they call home; flying serpents with pixie features, spiritual humans invited into the naga realm to study sacred wisdom and power and bring it back to the human world to teach and share. She sensed the presence of Divine Beings of non-human origin. One word popped into her brain – angels. Hungrily, she searched. There were none around but their loving, healing vibes were close by. There were also many like her, human hybrids with human shape and form decked in naga skins. There were various other earthly creatures merged with naga genes.

Cosmopolitan at its weirdest and best…

It was mind-boggling.

Immediately Anitha recognised one. "Ebony! Is that you?" Her mind relayed.

A luminous black cat with a long, twirling tail and moss-green scales for skin meandered expertly towards Anitha and licked her scales.

"Oh, you pretty little thing!" cooed Anitha, wordlessly, tracing her fingers across Ebony's scales. They played together for a while before Anitha heard her grandmother in her mind, urging her to take a left turn at the fork in the river. Ebony followed behind.

As she turned left, the feeling of being in the same space as angels intensified. The feeling of love here was so overwhelming and unbearable that her heart cried.

Here, the aquatic groves were thicker and denser and

intimately secluded. Radiant galaxies of mathematical configurations blinked on and off. Anitha was aware of the angelic power radiating from these geometric forms. She was struck by the concurrent flow of these angelic energies and the energies of suffering sickness, sorrow and trauma.

Numerous Nagas and Naga hybrids were resting, recuperating. Others were preparing for their passing, hopefully into higher realms. Many displayed outer proof of disabilities: damaged scales, blinded eyes, broken or missing limbs, diseased skins...others were ill in their minds and spirits. Each patient was snugly wrapped in a brilliant Light of Compassion.

"This is where we tend the sick and dying. Some are healed, some we care for till it is their time to leave their physical form and others come here to pass on peacefully."

It was the kindest, most loving voice Anitha had ever heard.

It was not her grandmother's. The speaker in her head was a simple white Naga with moonstone-encrusted white eyes. He continued, "The numbers keep increasing. All the elements of the earth are polluted resulting in all sorts of sicknesses. The waters of the earth are our lifeline. It is our home. It is here we live and love. The waters are the gateway through which we travel between dimensions."

"I am so sorry," Anitha wept in her heart.

Sliding towards her, the white Naga hugged her tenderly in his coil. "My dear, would you like to visit your mother?"

"My mother? She is here?"

The white naga directed her attention to a nearby grove where pulses of starry lights flickered in even intervals. "Beings from Higher Planes are working their healing on her."

Anxiously, Anitha swam towards her mother. She did not expect to see her mother in Naga form. In her very sick Naga form…

In deep slumber, on a bed of lotuses, stretched a serpent of approximately nine feet long. Mould blighted the dark blue scales. Bald patches where scales should have been made her look vulnerable, unprotected. A Circle of Stars around her came on and off like a switch. Floral and herbal fragrances wafted in the space.

"Ma…" Anitha tried to get nearer.

"She's resting." The white Naga flicked his tail gently at Anitha, preventing her from getting too close. "It is not advisable to wake her up. Her emotions and mind need a break. Fret not. She's in good hands."

Anitha lingered a while, just staring at her mother. "I love you, mum," she whispered.

There was nothing else she could do.

CHAPTER TWENTY-ONE

"She's coming round, Miss Tara."

"Come, hand me the towel and robe."

Fluttering her eyelids, Anitha was met with hazy images and sounds. Her human consciousness came to the surface. Her skin sensed the feel of grass and dew. She woke up. The sun was just peeping out. The first chirp of birdsong in the chilled air of dawn.

Her grandmother and Mira were watching over her. A towel and a white robe were handed to her. "Here. Dry yourself and slip on the robe. Mira has made banana pancakes for breakfast, and I like mine hot, so please get dressed!"

Anitha realised her nakedness as she rose from the banks of the river. She stumbled with dizziness. Mira caught her in time. Anitha ran her fingers across her skin – all human, no serpent scales.

Vague memories in the naga realm played in her head. She remembered her grandmother telling her it was time to return. She tried protesting. It had felt natural to be in that realm. She loathed having to leave this other home. Besides she did not wish to be apart from her mother.

"You have been here long enough." Her grandmother's warning had rung alarm bells in her ear.

As the first break of dawn unfolded, Anitha realised they had been away for an entire day.

It was the tastiest pancake ever. The hint of coconut and black pepper raised the pancakes to a whole new heavenly level.

Anitha had so many questions but for now her concern lay with her mother.

"She will be fine. In a week's time she will be ready to return to York." Her grandmother leaned against her chair, rubbing her tummy, satisfied with the meal.

"A week? But we're booked for two weeks!"

"And a week has just passed."

Dumbfounded, Anitha opened her mouth.

"Time travels differently in different dimensions."

"A week!" exclaimed Anitha.

"Yes. A week. All right, now, do you have any questions?"

"Loads..."

"Pick one that bothers you the most…"

"Will I find someone who can love me for…" Anitha tucked into her third pancake solemnly. She did not dare complete the question.

"For who you are…that depends…in the naga realm, you should have no problems but if it is a human boy you are considering…you will need all the strength to deal with the situation."

"Grandma…"

"Yes, sweetheart."

"Did dad know…did mum tell…?"

"No," came the blunt reply. "I advised her to be truthful from the beginning but she was already in love and afraid to lose him. They married and soon your mum discovered she was with you."

"Was dad happy?"

"I'd never seen a happier, prouder man. He was over the moon. You were the most precious gift in his life. As a matter of fact, every moment he had he spent with you."

"So…dad died not knowing about mum…"

There was no answer.

"Grandma!"

"Anitha…" her grandmother slowed her words. "On the day of the accident, your father had seen your mother shedding. For years, she had managed to keep it a secret. I don't know how she did it but she did.

Unfortunately, on that day, there was no hiding. She was caught off guard in the bath. Your father, being human, reacted by grabbing you and getting into the car and driving off. It was his human way of protecting his daughter from what he perceived to be a monstrous threat. He was not in the right frame of mind nor emotion to be behind the wheel."

For minutes, Anitha did not say anything. Her head was hot, her heart was thumping and once again, that old, familiar hate and anger began its journey through her blood. "Why? Why didn't mum tell me all these years?" Anitha burst violently. "She's a liar! I hate her!"

Anitha's grandmother rushed to her side and cradled her in her arms. "What was my child supposed to say? That she killed him because she drove him to his death? She never forgave herself, Anitha, for that day…and it eats her everyday that you don't know the truth."

"I know now and I'll never forgive her! I hate her! Dad is dead because of her!" Her shoulders shook as she sobbed on her grandma's arms.

"Anitha, I feel your pain. I am so sorry for your loss."
Anitha mewled.

"Your mother is sick, Anitha. Every day she lives, she pays the price for that day. My daughter needs to forgive herself. Hopefully, one day, you too will forgive your mother…"

CHAPTER TWENTY-TWO

The lapis-lazuli blue of the scales gleamed in the bath. The afternoon light beaming from the bathroom window kissed yellow golden rays upon the

shape-shifting serpent immersed in the bath water.

Anitha spied her mother's nakedness waist-up, human and womanly, so desired by dad. Smiling, her mother turned to face her, reaching out her arms, beckoning Anitha to her.

Anitha stepped back. No, she mouthed, you lied to dad and you killed him and you lied to me…all these years!

Suddenly, her mother's face switched. Anitha screamed. She was looking at herself. Footsteps came up the landing. The door to the bathroom opened. Anitha saw the horror and fear in her father's eyes. She tried to explain but he did not listen. He could not.

Suddenly, her father's face faded. Solomon was now staring at her.

No! No! Anitha wailed. Frantically, she slithered out of the bath but it was too late. She heard him trip and stumble over the laundry basket and roll down the stairs.

At the landing, she saw his twisted body and dead eyes – open and accusing…

The dream returned the next night and the next. It was torment being inside her mother, her father, Solomon… but Anitha was finally beginning to get to grips with the wisdom of her dreams.

"Here, I made you some payasam for breakfast." Her grandmother pushed a dessert bowl towards her.

It had been three days since the truth of her dad had been revealed to her and three nights of the recurrent dream. There was less than a week to go before she bid goodbye to grandma. "Thanks but what is it?"

"Rice pudding made with coconut milk, raisins, nuts and seeds, and sweetened with honey. Decadent."

It was so decadent Anitha requested a second bowl.

"Let's go shopping. You haven't done anything touristy since your arrival."

"I think I've toured the best of Kerala. I want to spend time with you, gran, and the garden, and I need you to tell me what I need to know about who I am."

"That will take a lifetime. You will learn a lot on your own but you can help by being in tune with your naga element. Shall we take a walk in the garden?"

"Naga pattu simply means, naga song or serpent song. I hear you write very well."

"Sort of…just a few verses that I have filed away for years…"

She and her grandmother were seated on bamboo chairs in the garden where she had a comforting view of the sarpa kavu and The Well. They had just finished a leisurely stroll.

"You can, in your lazy moments, be inspired and compose poems connecting you to your serpent half. Usually, these songs are composed for and performed during traditional ritual and worship held at certain times of the year. I believe however that faith is a personal choice and how one chooses to express one's faith is nobody else's business."

Kumar appeared, grinning, carrying two coconuts with straws inserted through them. "Here, drink some coconut water. They are from your grandmother's groves."

"Thank you, Kumar." Anitha placed her coconut on the wooden garden table and took a sip of the cool, sweet drink. She could drink coconut water all day.

He placed a plate of steaming, spicy snacks on the table. "Mira fried these lotus-root fritters for you. Our children love these. You must sample."

Anitha bit into a slice of fried lotus root. The flavours of black pepper, chilli and rice flour danced on her tongue. "Goodness!"

"Do you like it?" Kumar creased his brows.

"Are you kidding?"

"I am not kidding, miss. I do not kid my wife's cooking. I am asking…"

"It's delicious! Tell her I would love to eat more!"

"She will be happy. I will tell her now. She will be happy." He disappeared into the kitchen.

"Kumar and Mira know, of course…" Anitha stuffed a few more fritters into her mouth.

"Of course. Well, back to you. Now that you have been initiated and undergone The Shedding, I would advise you to shed and slip into your naga skin each menstrual cycle. You can do it in the bath or in the river Ouse."

"How do I know I haven't disappeared for a week?"

"You will be aware. Your human side will tug at you. Listen to it. Don't worry."

Anitha finished her coconut water.

"Honour your shadows, Anitha. They are you. You can be your own worst enemy or nightmare if you hide them. Skeletons in the closet are no good to anyone. Give them a platform, a voice. Don't muffle or imprison them. Love all of you. Don't cherry pick. Every fibre of your being has meaning and relevance.

Remember, you are your Mother's daughter, Anitha. You are of Serpent Born."

Anitha felt she was running out of time. There was too much to know, to learn, to be. She didn't want to leave. "When will I see you again, grandma? When will I see you again?" She was welling up in tears.

"My dear, dear, dear, grandbaby girl, just think of me and I will be there with you."

And with those tender words stored carefully in her heart, this time the next week Anitha was back home in York.

CHAPTER TWENTY-THREE

Leaves of emerald green, copper red, rusty brown and lime-yellow infused with cinnabar-gold shots lifted themselves off trees, fluttering freely in mid-air before settling to nature's fate.

Raising her face to the autumnal breeze, Anitha allowed drifting leaves to paste her cheeks. Damp and fresh, they stuck on her skin like wet kisses. Laughing, Durga peeled them off.

Hand in hand, they trudged along the soggy nature trail at Rawcliffe Meadows. A few weeks had passed since their Kerala trip, Anitha's revelations and Durga's healing. Anitha was back in school and her bullies no longer bothered her. Despite not witnessing nor remembering her changing, they appeared spooked in her presence. In school, they avoided her like the plague.

The night before their departure from grandmother's

home, Durga emerged from The Well not the river as Anitha had done. Anitha did not ask why. She was just grateful to have her mother back. Although Durga was pale and thin, grandma assured her that she would improve with time, rest, healthy food and clean water.

They had hugged and wept and tucked into a hearty feast that Mira and grandma had prepared: dosas with dhal and a brinjal and a dish of okra cooked in tomatoes and seasoned with, of course, crushed black peppercorns, the black gold of Kerala. Finally, for dessert and late-night savoury snacks, Mira served up creamy mango pudding sweetened with rice syrup, sprinkled with pistachios and nutmeg, and her famous spicy lotus fritters specially for Anitha.

"Mum, Miss Devon was so impressed with my fracking project that she asked me to do a ten-minute presentation next week in front of the class."

"You deserved that 'A'. Are you nervous?"

"Yes."

"We'll practise together, all right?"

"I'd like that."

"Shall we turn back now?" Durga pulled her scarf over her mouth and blew into it. "We'll grab a hot drink in the city and shop for some Halloween decorations at the one-pound shop."

"Mum, it's weeks away."

"And time flies...you should know...anyway, I am

proud you are helping out at the village hall for the Halloween children's party."

"Well, I thought why not instead of being stuck in a rut and staying at home like every other year."

Durga trod carefully with her next few words. "It's ideal to meet new people...yes?"

They walked back, past the Clifton Ings with its sprawling fields of meadows.

"I was thinking, mum, of volunteering with the Rawcliffe Meadows Society."

"That's great. They could do with all the support."

"Well, yes," teased Anitha, "Mother Nature told me that she would love to breed more tansy beetles.

"She did now, did she?"

"Jealous?"

"You cheeky monkey..."

Anitha mopped the last of her hot parsnip and butternut squash soup with seeded gluten-free bread. Pellets of dark, cold rain beat against the dining room window. She heard her mother run the bath. Within seconds, there was the fragrance of ylang ylang and rose permeating the air.

Her mother was preparing to shed.

It was her time of the month.

The recurrent dream of her switching places with her mum in the bath and Solomon switching places with her dad had ceased. She didn't need the lesson any more. She had been in their skins and understood why everything happened the way it did.

Mum did not have to hide any more.

CHAPTER TWENTY-FOUR

October 31st

Halloween Party, Village Hall

Witches and ghouls, vampires and ghosts, zombies and superheroes, gods and angels all gyrated to Rihanna's "…lightning strikes every time she moves. Everybody's watching her but she's looking at you hoo, hoo hoo hoo, you hoo, hoo, hoo, hoo…"

The disco ball swung, beaming flashes of rainbow colours on the crowded dance floor magnifying the non-human masks and costumes with cinematic effect. The party was clearly a success attracting residents from the surrounding villages. The parish council had advertised it on Facebook hoping to inject some life into the otherwise tranquil, rural village by welcoming children and young people from the neighbouring areas. Anitha had seen her name on the list of volunteers along with…Solomon's.

"May I please have a punch, miss?" It was a five-year old girl with a hairy wolf head. Her breath was uneven from all the dancing.

An older boy stood over her. Dressed in black jeans and t-shirt, he warned her, "Not too much, Celia. I don't want to take you to the loo every five minutes."

"Strawberry or apple, sweetie?" Anitha enquired.

"I'm not a sweetie. I'm a werewolf. Raaa!" she roared. "Strawberry, please."

Faking a fearful expression, Anitha handed her the cup of punch with trembling hands. The little girl took it with her paws, delighted to have terrified someone.

"Don't drink it all at once, will you?" Her brother led her away to the rows of chairs lined against the walls where they sat for a few minutes before hopping onto the dance floor.

Tapping her feet to the rhythm of the music, Anitha noticed some mothers giggling in a group, sipping their punch while keeping an eye on their children. One of the women pulled out a flask from her bag and tipped a bit of its contents into each of her companions' cup. Older boys and girls huddled in secret circles, chatting, texting and sharing pictures on their mobiles. There were some dads standing around conversing while drinking punch and eating the finger food. At least they looked sober.

And then there were the clowns – three of them wearing hideous blood-soaked, grinning white masks sitting in a corner with their fake axes and not saying a word to one another.

"Need any help?"

Anitha jumped.

Solomon poured himself a punch. "Tasty…"

"My mum made it – all natural and organic."

"Good idea. What's the point of having fun when you are sick the next day?"

Anitha reverted her attention to the clowns.

"Creepy aren't they?" Solomon mumbled.

Anitha nodded.

"How was your trip to Kerala?"

"Good."

"Listen…I'm…I don't know what to say but that day…"

"It's all right. You don't have to explain, Solomon. I understand. I don't expect you to."

"Anitha…that day…what I saw…happening to you…"

"This is not the time, Solomon. Maybe another day… another time…or maybe not at all?"

Sighing, Solomon acquiesced. "Can I at least walk you back home after the party? Ebony's with me."

The boy was trying. "I'd like that," Anitha said.

And she meant it.

CHAPTER TWENTY-FIVE

Huddled in their parkas, woollen scarves and gloved hands in pockets, Anitha and Solomon waved goodbye to the children and chaperones and the other volunteers at the village hall gates.

"Thank you for volunteering." Sally, one of the committee members hugged Anitha and Solomon. "What a lovely turnout. It's drizzling. Need a lift, you two?"

They both shook their heads.

"No thanks, Sally. I'm just five minutes away." Anitha pulled her hood over her head. Secretly, she hoped the walk would be really slow and take longer.

"Good night, then. Hurry home. It's too dark and chilly and wet to be out too long. " Winking, Sally revved up her car engine and drove off.

Save for the rain hitting the pavement, the night

was quiet. The sky was empty of stars and the waning moon was hidden in veils of foggy shadows.

Ebony purred.

Anitha bent to stroke the cat.

"Shall we? We don't want your mum worrying." Solomon blew mist from his breath.

"You're right. Thanks. You can come in for hot cocoa, if you want…"

"You sure?"

"Of course. Just call your grandparents. You don't want them worrying."

They laughed and walked out of Vicar Lane where at the crossroads an old yew tree stood, gnarled and crooked. Anitha noted its slithering roots and branches, a labyrinth of twisted vines resembling serpents.

Her heart leapt.

Solomon, her secret…it was all too soon, too complicated…

They passed the pub, The Blacksmith's Arms, still noisy and busy with

late-night Halloween patrons headed towards the slipway. The river flowed with silvery ripples. She paused to stare.

"The rain's coming down hard, Anitha. Come on," Solomon urged impatiently, tugging her left hand.

Anitha let herself be held. His gloved fingers slipped through hers securely. His breath was warm and moist.

Her body simmered with heat.

The night was theirs.

Ebony growled with her fur erect and her mouth peeled back, baring teeth.

"What is it, Ebony?" Solomon released his grip.

Three figures appeared opposite the pub, their garish clown masks uglier under the orange light of the street lamp. They were still as statues.

An owl hooted. The winds picked speed. Rain belted down.

"Run, Anitha." Solomon's command was low and deep.

Ebony's yowling pitch rose.

Anitha did not run.

One of the figures, the shorter one of the three, pointed its comical bulbous, bloodied forefinger at Anitha. It was a cue for the other two to start running crazily towards Anitha.

"Run Anitha!" yelled Solomon as he launched himself towards one of the clowns, wrestling it to the ground.

Ebony flew to claw the other opponent. It was too late. The clown kicked Ebony and swung the fake axe at the animal. It was no fake axe but a bat. Instantly, Ebony crumpled, landing on the riverbank. Hurling Anitha to the ground, he, clearly a male, slapped her hard on her face. Her cheeks cracked. The pain stung. She heard menacing female laughter coming from the clown directing the assault.

"Have fun, boys," she goaded.

Struggling to push her assailant off, Anitha recognised the voice. "Uma?" Uma.

"Happy Halloween."

"Uma! Make him stop! Please!" Anitha pleaded, breathlessly. The clown on top of her ripped the zip off her parka and was viciously pulling down her jeans.

"You didn't think I was going to let you off that easy, did you?" Uma spat, her clown mask tilting to one side. "Trick or treat? I thought I'd give the boys a treat," she said coldly.

Distressed, Anitha, glanced frantically sideways. She saw Solomon punching and being punched. His nose was bleeding and his eyes swelled with fresh bruises. However, he was taller and bigger – there was life in him yet.

On the riverbank, lay Ebony, her breath ragged, her little black body twitching for its life.

Anitha's blood surged feverishly.

Her body juddered.

Her skin grew hot and cold.

The Changing.

It was happening.

CHAPTER TWENTY-SIX

Lightning knifed across the black, starless sky splitting it in a thunderous roar. Screeching winds swept in billowing shadows. The slipway rumbled. Hypnotised, the boys stopped open-mouthed, their eyes fixed on Anitha.

She hissed, her forked tongue slithering venomously at the quaking clown pressed upon her sinewy, scaled body. Whimpering, he scrambled backwards, his legs helplessly glued to the ground. He was no further than a few yards away from the crystalline human creature that now emerged on its feet, glowing in a circle of unearthly, resplendent light. Blinding, white micro-crystal scales studded her Gorgon's tresses. Her entire face and body, clad in layers of crystal-serpent scales, emitted showers of electric sparks. Mercurial, slanted eyes of fiery gold danced with dangerous elation.

Anitha hissed, her fangs, dripping with poison. With a single leap, she crushed upon her attacker on all fours and bit him. Swiftly, she hurled herself upon the remaining petrified assailant, sinking her fangs into him. In a split second, Anitha met Solomon's eyes. Their gazes tangled. She hissed. He did not move an inch.

A shriek alerted her. It was Uma, running for her life in her clown suit. Hissing, Anitha leapt, slithering in mid-air like a wingless predator, landing on Uma. She pushed her to the ground, finishing off her prey with the spit of her venom.

And then, it happened.

A grave quietness dropped like a guillotine.

Winds wailed ghoulishly. Weeping willows by the banks of the slipway thrashed and swayed. Stabs of lightning cracked the skies in shattering splinters. The Ouse churned. It churned and swirled and rose like a liquid hurricane, bringing up with it bones and weeds and scales. Shadows moaned incantations.

"Anitha!" Solomon cried.

Anitha hissed, her hybrid cells vibrating violently inside her. She rushed towards the river as the rising waters sketched a faint outline of a cobra.

The Mother.

Anitha turned to pick Ebony up from the muddy

banks. She spun round to glimpse Solomon. A tidal wave shrouded her, swallowing her into its watery tomb.

The waters received her. Ebony was close to her chest. Pinging sounds reverberated through the ripples. It was dark and peaceful in the river. Her rage dissolved as she flowed with the currents.

"Anitha…"

Anitha did not wish to be disturbed.

"Anitha…"

"Grandma?"

"Anitha…"

"Grandma! Grandma! Am…Am…am I dead?"

"Silly girl! You are very much alive. It is not your time."

"Go away, Grandma." Anitha clutched Ebony possessively.

"Anitha, you need to return and remove the poisons immediately."

"I will not. They deserved it. Get out of my head."

"Hate is not the way. Do not abuse your nature. Our venom is the cure. Love, Anitha, only love heals."

"Ebony…what about Ebony? Will she be all right?"

"We will assist her on her journey."

Anitha kissed the furry beast.

"Anitha, you are your Mother's daughter. Love

gave birth to you. Return in love. Go. Time is of the essence."

After one last cuddle, Anitha opened her arms and released Ebony to the waters.

She was surprised to see Solomon sitting by the banks. The rain had stopped. The winds had died down. "I had a feeling you'd come back."

Her scales glistened wetly. "Whatever."

"Ebony?"

Anitha shook her head solemnly. Solomon restrained his emotions. "It took me a while but I called the ambulance. It should be here any minute. I felt it was the right thing to do."

"You did the right thing." Anitha went to each of the clowns, removing their masks. The boys were her cousins, her father's nephews from his eldest sister. They were dying.

A few drunken vampire revellers whistled as they stumbled out of the pub. "Great costume!"

"What are you going to do?" Solomon asked.

"I'm going to re-bite them with my venom. It activates the anti-bodies in their immune system creating the anti-venom." Anitha heard the ambulance.

"Why?"

"Because it is the right thing to do."

CHAPTER TWENTY-SEVEN

December

Dark Moon

"It's already ten, Anitha. Time for bed. We have a long day tomorrow. The sentencing is at nine in the morning after which we'll see granddad in hospital."

Surya and Sunder were found guilty of aggravated assault with intent to cause harm. They had stalked her on Facebook, tracking her whereabouts. Their sentence was to be read tomorrow. As for Uma, she was to be tried in juvenile court. Her case was still under investigation.

None of the three remembered her transformation. They recalled the Halloween party and confessed to the attack at the slipway but after that, they woke up to the ambulance and the police handcuffing them.

The paramedics attended to Solomon and Anitha,

both marked with blood and bruises, and broken bones

"Yes, mum. I'm just finishing something off."

"What are you doing?"

"A naga pattu."

"A naga pattu?"

"Yes, a serpent song. Grandma said composing a song or poetry in honour of my naga line will help me connect to it in a healing way."

"When I was growing up, I used to attend festivals where a naga pattu was sung and performed. They were very grand with feasting, music, dancing and hours of pujas," Durga recalled. "Only women and girls were entitled to perform the sarpam thullal, the serpent dance. I'm glad you are keeping the tradition alive in your own, personal way."

"Mum, what will happen when granddad's gone?"

"I promise you, we will have nothing to do with dad's family and I am sure they would want nothing to do with us. We can shed them from our lives and begin anew. Now finish off and come to bed."

Anitha waited for her mum to go upstairs. There was something else that was snagging her brain.

Solomon. Everyone who had witnessed her changing could not remember it except for Solomon. He remembered everything. They had not spoken since that Halloween night and had simply exchanged hellos at the court trials.

He wasn't ready to talk.

She wasn't going to impose.

Sometimes, life is best left to its own unfolding.

That night, in the deep, dark waters of her dreams, Anitha, in all her crystal glory, swam with cats and moons, angels and stars and serpents and shadows...

...freely...

...lovingly...

...eternally...

Naga pattu (Serpent Song)
Composed by Anitha

Naga Mata
❧

Shedding
renewing
death
rebirth
dark moon
full moon
sunset
sunrise
neither beginning nor ending
The Womb
The Grave
Seasons and
cycles
Infinite
Immortal…
She
The Mother

The Nag Panchami is a sacred festival for many Hindus across India. Panchami stands for 5 and this holy festival is celebrated on the 5th day of the waxing moon during the lunar months of July/August. Nag Panchami is held in honour/worship of Serpent Deities and Divine Blessings are invoked for the benefit of the family, community and the fertility of the land so all can prosper and co-exist symbiotically. There are diverse and unique ways in which this festival is celebrated, some of which include, fasting, chanting mantras, offering of milk and rice pudding, dancing and creating art forms of Serpents.

Also published by Ragged Bears

Heart Of Resistance

Sarah Tate

A story of survival against the odds.

When a bomb destroys her London home, Agnes is left without parents or a guardian. But she can't bear to live in a children's home in the country. She needs to find her grandparents in France – a France occupied by the Nazis.

Smuggled across the Channel, by chance she meets a Resistance group whose leader promises to help her in her quest. In turn, Agnes's quick-thinking saves both of them. Left in care of shepherds in the mountains, Agnes' adventure is only just beginning…

ISBN: 9781857144277

Find us online
at
ragged-bears.com

 @BooksBears

 /raggedbears

 raggedbears